A Bad Winter

Samantha Priestley

To

Margaret

Best wish

SL

A Ghostly Tale

Published by Armley Press 2017
ISBN 978-0-9934811-7-8

Acknowledgements
Copy-editing: John Lake
Layout: Ian Dobson
Production: Mick McCann
Cover design: Mick Lake
Cover art: William Hallett

For Wil, Eva and Lily

ALSO BY SAMANTHA PRIESTLEY
Despite Losing It on Finkle Street
Dreamers
Reliability of Rope
Orange Balloon

A Bad Winter

Sometime in the 1760s this happened in Derbyshire

The snow had fallen the day before and tonight, a slow wind curling in the valley, all about was frozen. Sarah approached the house, pulling at her skirts as a cold branch snagged her from behind. The branch held on for the briefest moment, brittle claws tugging, but lost its fight as Sarah pulled herself free. Only the light from a shaded moon helped her forward.

Her feet slid on humps of frozen snow. She could feel the places his feet had walked earlier in the day, the warmth from the roots of his body melting curves in the frozen ground, and hers, making ice bump like the clods of earth in the top field. Sarah tried to figure the path in front of her, but her feet lost their way a couple of times and the soles of her shoes failed and slipped on the blackness of the ice.

She saw the front door of the house open, yellow light behind his bulky form as he stepped out. She heard him speak to the dog and a whistle fly from his lips as the dog jumped and ran in the cold night.

"Bess, 'ere!"

Sarah stopped dead and waited, her arms slightly apart from her body to steady herself. The door closed and Joseph walked quickly away from the house.

It was the dog who found her first. Bess's warm nose snorting breath forward in the dark, her brown eyes shining as she caught the scent of Sarah waiting down by the bush. The dog leapt at the girl, her hind legs skitting on the frozen ground, her front paws up and muddying Sarah's clothes. Sarah put her fingers to the place behind Bess's ears and rubbed them like lumps of butter in flour.

"Bess," she whispered. "My girl, yer know me, alright, don't yer?"

Joseph was only three strides behind the dog and he came upon them like he was the deceived and they were the lovers.

"Bess!" he said, and he yanked the dog away from Sarah. Then he stood himself tall and looked down on the girl. "Sarah," he said. "Tis a cold night."

"Aye, that it is," she replied, a smile beginning, "but I'm the one to warm yer on this cold night, Joseph."

She saw something enter his eyes then, like she often did. Sarah encouraged herself to mistake it for emotion, a shift under his skin, a heat in his body, which he could never turn away from. But it was more animal than anything Sarah had ever seen in Bess's eyes.

Joseph turned Sarah away from him, the top of her head resting beneath his breastbone, and urged her into the wooded area behind his house. It meant them turning back towards the solid stone house, smoke like a wisp of hair from the chimney, the light from the fire inside golden on the windows. Then away to the right they moved, away to the trees. Sarah giggled. Joseph's arm fitted around her waist, his other hand up under her skirts. He had her by a tree, neither the house below them nor the path above them visible from where they stood. Her skirts high around her waist, Joseph's breath hot by her face. A quick fumbling with his clothes and she felt herself lifted a little more.

Bess began to bark, frosted leaves brittle beneath her set paws. Bits of bark from the tree fell to the ground around Sarah's back.

When she felt Joseph's body relax against her and his shoulders slump, Sarah opened her eyes. Through the pattern of the trees she could see, up on the top of the hill, the shape of cattle slow in the cold evening, black against the winter sky. They hardly moved at all, their bulky forms meandering like streams. She lifted her head slightly and above she saw the moon, shimmering beneath the clouds like its own reflection on water. The cattle shifted in the corner of her eye, the moon bright on her face, and she thought she saw a different form flit behind the animals up on the hill. But it was gone, if it was there at all. Joseph removed his body and Sarah fell to a standing position by the tree, her clothes ruffling against her legs as they dropped back into place.

Joseph stood back, fastening his clothes again. He bent, his face taut, and he grabbed at a lump of frozen snow on the ground, holding it in his fist, so cold it burned. He threw it with such force it made Sarah flinch, though it wasn't aimed in her direction. She could feel all his frustration and aggression exiting his body with that one angry action. He threw it at a space between the trees to his right and watched for just a second as it scattered and hit the ground in lumps. Then he looked at her. "There's trouble," he said. "Standing right there and looking like Sarah Vernon. There's trouble alright."

"I'll be no trouble to you, Joseph," she said.

"This shun't go on," he said. "We 'ave the devil in us when we do this."

"And yet it does go on," she said.

He looked to the side, away from her face, and watched the dog sniffing amongst the icy leaves. He moved suddenly, like he always did, without a moment for Sarah to complain. "'Ere Bess!" he said, and he walked back down towards the house.

*

Joseph walked down past the house where his wife sat mending by the fire, down, Bess trotting by his heels, down past the bush where Sarah had waited, watching the house till he came out, down, walking in the lane with Bess close and his thoughts even closer. Then after thinking he had to put a stop to it, but feeling the failing in his body already and knowing he could do nothing to stop himself, down he went, down the path to the Kingston Arms, the "Low Drop" as it was better known. Joseph entered the Kingston Arms, stepping down, the floor of the inn lower than the ground outside its door, giving the place its pet name. The inn keeper looked up. Joseph was quickly aware of a silence settling like soft early winter snow. He looked around, caught the side glances and the mutters of drinkers as they avoided his eyes.

The inn keeper cocked his head. "Joseph," he said. "You'll find no favour in 'ere tonight. 'Appen yer should go 'ome."

Joseph blew out a laugh with a question lifting in it.

"To yer wife," the inn keeper put in.

Joseph was about to ask what he meant by this when he

became aware of a disturbance to his left. Mr Vernon's neighbour, George, was on his feet, almost knocking over the low table he sat by, two other men standing also and holding him back.

"You!" George shouted, his hand held out in front of him, his finger pointing right at Joseph. "You show yer face in 'ere!"

The other men tried to calm him. Joseph stood for a moment, anger dividing inside him, Bess sitting by his feet, wagging her tail. He felt his guilt wriggle through and bring red to his face. They didn't know. They didn't know. But he couldn't stand here now and face them. They didn't know, did they? How could they know? How? He turned as quickly as he had on Sarah up by the tree, and he stepped up and out of the Low Drop.

*

Sarah was walking down the lane, her skirts white in the dark evening, when Joseph was on his way back up. She held her skirts and swayed them in the air about her legs as he came upon her. She was smiling. He took her by the neck and forced her backwards. Such strength in his arm, he could almost carry her by the throat like that, and she felt her heels being dragged along the ground as she was pushed backwards. She pulled at his arm with her hands, but she was tiny next to him. Bess stood in the lane and barked.

"Who did yer tell?" Joseph's voice came out between his barred teeth, his hot breath in the cold air right upon her face.

She tried to shake her head.

"Yer surely din't tell yer father, did yer? Yer a bigger fool than I am if yer did."

She shook her head again, her eyes pleading with him, her hand trying hopelessly to loosen his on her neck.

He shook her, her long brown hair flying around her head. "Yer father's neighbour were in't Low Drop just now, looking at me like he'd as soon as kill me. I know yer told."

He shook her again. He'd forced her back to the dry-stone wall that ran the edge of the middle field.

10

"What, did yer tell him before yer came out tonight?" he urged. "Did yer plan it? What y'after, girl? Money? I'd rather kill yer than give yer money."

Sarah strained her eyes to her right and could see the fire burning inside Joseph's house now. His wife would be sitting there, thinking he was walking Bess and calling at the Kingston Arms, laughing and drinking with the other men. If he'd let go of her neck, Sarah would tell him how she loved him, how he invaded her dreams at night, how his image chased her thoughts all through every day, how all that meant anything to her was when she would next see him. She would give him her heart and he would surely understand. But Joseph didn't let go. He gripped her neck and she could see, as the moon shone behind her, the look in his eyes, more fierce than when he took her quickly in his arms, more urgent. Joseph's great form was upon her as he forced her down right next to the chaotic jagged wall, slab after slab of misshapen stone. Sarah put her hands behind her and felt the sharp edges of the stone near the ground. She felt frantically about until her fingers found the cold softness of snow on the grass. Joseph shook her again. "Who did yer tell?" he shouted. "Who knows?"

In the darkness it was hard for Joseph to see how close Sarah's head was to the stone wall, but as he shook her violently and shouted his questions at her, he felt the muffled, heavy sound of her head hitting the sharp stones beneath her. He kept his hand fixed around her neck for a moment, staring into her still face. "Sarah!" he hissed, shaking her again. But this time she couldn't respond. As he shook her body by her neck he saw the black sticky liquid on the stone behind her, matted in the hair at the back of her head, and drops melting red into the snow beneath. "Sarah!" he whispered again.

*

Bess was barking at his heels as he stood up and looked down on Sarah. He'd let her fall to the ground and now his fingers worried his mouth as he felt his tongue dry. He motioned with his head to Bess without taking his eyes off Sarah. "Shush

11

now, Bess!" The dog moved forward and pushed her nose into the still folds of Sarah's skirts. "Away, Bess!" he snapped. Joseph looked up at the house and saw the light of the fire inside. Beyond that he could see the woods and the edge of the hill against the night sky. He bent quickly and scooped Sarah up in his arms, then he carried her behind the house and up into the woods.

He left her for just a moment while he fetched a shovel, and it was the only time since he'd known Sarah that he felt the parting at all. Each second he was away from her still body, worry trembled in him. Bess stayed with Sarah, the briefest shift in the dog's loyalty, Joseph thought. But when he returned he saw that the dog was keeping watch and remained obedient to Joseph all along. She stood up and barked when Joseph came back with the shovel in his hands.

Bess was still barking when Joseph began to dig in the earth between the trees. He felt the fear that someone would hear the dog and question it, but he shushed her every now and then and worked quickly. Eventually Bess seemed to tire, and lay down amongst the leaves on the frozen ground. It was tough work – the winter earth had a hard crust he had to break and the digging didn't get much easier till the earth beneath became softer. Halfway through, Joseph felt cold sleet fall on him. He stopped for a moment and stood up straight, turning his face to the sky and feeling the sleet hit his skin. He caught sight of Sarah from the corner of his eye, her hair tangling with leaves and mud, her face speckled with sleet and earth. He'd stopped, and the quiet seemed to settle. Only the patter of the sleet finding a surface. Then a rustle of leaves and Bess up on her legs again, barking, but not at Joseph or Sarah this time. Joseph looked at the dog, her face fixed on a place behind Joseph, her eyes shining in the night and her teeth bared slightly. Joseph turned and saw a figure between the trees, dark in the slope of the hill, the house behind. It was only a moment, no longer than a single breath. A black outline of a person, a crack of twigs and brittle leaves as he or she saw Joseph turn and shifted amongst the trees to get away. Bess still barked, but between the trees the figure moved like fog, and was gone.

*

Anne was sitting close to the fire. She could feel the heat infusing her face and making her drowsy. A couple of times the fabric and the needle and thread in her hands dropped like snow from a branch. She could feel her eyes close and her body give, sleep pulling at her. She always waited for Joseph. When she married him her mother told her she should always be careful and make sure the two of them went to their bed together.

"Men 'ave wandering minds," her mother had said. "It's up to you to make sure 'is stays right there with you. Don't give 'im the chance to be thinking, now. If 'e's taken a drink, which 'e mostly will 'ave, 'im being the way, yer must still wait for 'im to come 'ome, now. 'E'll want 'is way, but at least with the drink in 'im it will be over quick."

Anne had looked at her mother as if she was mad. Joseph was a good man. Not a man of many words, but a good, God-fearing man. The things her mother talked of were surely for some other poor woman's ears.

"Always go to the bed together," her mother said, dropping her voice and lowering her eyes. "If yer grow tired waiting for 'im to come in and yer already asleep, he will 'appen be angry. That's when a man starts to think, and yer don't want that – ycr want his mind right 'ere," and she prodded her daughter's chest hard.

So Anne always waited for him. She would sit and mend or stare into the leap of the fire, at the way it sent flicks of itself out and caught the old sword Joseph kept propped up by the hearth. And when Joseph came in she would have some supper waiting for him, which he sometimes ate and sometimes didn't.

But tonight he was later than usual. Anne had heard Bess barking about an hour or so ago and had expected the dog to come padding through the door when Joseph opened it, his large form filling the gap. But they didn't appear and Anne found herself listening for every sound out in the night, beginning to worry.

When Anne had married Joseph, her mother's warnings and advice had seemed ludicrous. Joseph was a serious man. He loved her. She would never have to mind him. But lately Anne had begun to feel a discomfort. Something wasn't right. He was distracted. Anne couldn't say what it was, but the usual nodding thought of another woman shifted around in the forefront of her brain. He would drink in the Low Drop, then come home, Anne waiting for him by the fire, and he would look at her then carry on up to bed, without saying a word. He was never one for talking, but he was always one for actions. Now he didn't even do much of that, just looked at Anne and then went to bed and slept, his snores filled with beer and who knows what else. Anne knew there was something. If she was honest with herself, she knew there was someone.

When the door finally opened and he stood there, the night making him a shadow, Bess leaping in and lying down by the fire, Anne was sure of it.

Today

Lorraine hated the winter. Except for the clothes she could wear. Except for knee-high boots and fur-collared coats. The tight jeans and the tighter sweaters. And her breath in the cold morning air, coming out like a horse's breath, like the ones she'd seen in closed fields as a kid and had dreamed of riding and owning, but never had. Sometimes she'd sneaked down to the field's edge after school and had stood and beckoned a horse over. Her hand had gently shaped the side of its head, its breath blurting from its nose like steam from a covered pan. She still liked that. Still liked to let the memory roll around inside her. Even though the horse was never Lorraine's horse, was only on loan to her for the moments she spent there. Like everything. Like everyone.

Mostly, Lorraine hated the way the weather in winter made everything so difficult. Just walking was difficult. Black ice like a sheen of top-coat on her nails. You couldn't see it, couldn't tell it was there, couldn't identify its purpose by looking, because it was deceptive. You only knew it was there when you touched it or the light caught it at a certain angle and you could see it shine. Otherwise, it encased what was beneath it and it kept quiet. And usually you slipped on it and ended up on your arse.

Lorraine really hated the winter. It was cold. It was miserable. She said so to Glenn when he picked her up in his car.

"It's bloody freezing," she said. "Have you got the heater on in here?"

Glenn checked the settings inside his BMW, then moulded her knee with his hand. "Don't worry, babe," he said. "I'll soon warm you up."

She smiled. It really was ridiculous how much she liked it when he said things like that. Glenn was the kind of guy who, in Lorraine's opinion, kept a stacked-up pile of sayings and phrases and effective single words which he could leaf through in his brain whenever he needed them. He didn't pay much of a toll when he sped through all these words and phrases. Probably didn't think too much about them at all. Certainly didn't mean many of them. But he knew they worked. He knew they got him what he wanted.

Anyway, Lorraine didn't mind. She understood the game. And Glenn always gave her what she wanted too.

She looked around nervously as Glenn leaned in to kiss her, his hand rolling on her knee.

"Nobody can see," he said quietly. She grinned and then followed his lean and kissed him.

Of course somebody could have seen. Any of her neighbours could easily have seen. That's why Glenn always picked her up round the corner from her house. Never in full view. Never too obvious. But, still, all the people on this next street knew who Lorraine was anyway, and they could have seen.

She gave him the moment. Knew there was a part of this deception and intrigue that turned him on. He'd said so. He'd actually said so once. After he'd dropped her off one night in the rain and she'd had to walk from the end of the street to her house, Glenn saying, "It's a good thing anyway – If you turned up home all dry, he'd wonder. This way you'll be wet and it will look like you've walked from the bus stop." He'd texted her and told her it turned him on, the creeping about, the lying, the barely hidden looks and kissing in the car when anyone might see.

Of course, they never sailed so close around his house. Oh, no. They never came within a sniff of his street. Never so much as gave a glance to the area he lived in. That would have been too risky, Glenn said. That would have been irresponsible and stupid.

But Lorraine didn't mind. She had her eye on what she was doing. Didn't she?

She kept her face close to his as the kiss came to an end. "Are we going somewhere or what?" she asked.

"Of course, angel," he replied.

She sat up straight, quickly glanced around again for possible busybodies. And Glenn turned the key and the engine started.

A Bad Winter

Derbyshire, 1760s

He stood there for a moment, his black form in the doorway sending a strange fear through Anne. She wasn't scared of the man, of Joseph, but of whatever it was he was bringing to her now.

Slowly he closed the door behind him and made his way over to the fire. Anne could see he was cold, shivering, and he knelt down and held his hands together in front of the flames as if he was praying. He moved his hands slightly to warm them, then he looked at Anne. She tensed, waiting.

"Somert's 'appened, lass," he said. "Somert bad, and I don't know 'ow... or what."

Anne had never seen her husband break in this way before. He was a strong man. He showed little emotion in his day-to-day life and the sight of him now, the fear in his face, alarmed her. For a moment, she was afraid. For a moment, she wanted none of this. Wanted him to go back outside and come in again a different Joseph. The one she was used to. Then a scurry of thoughts ran in her head and made a change brew in her chest. This was her way back to him. If she stood by him now and helped him where she could, he would see, he would love her again. And her love took over. He needed her right now. Maybe more than he ever had; certainly, more than he had for a long while now. She reached out and took his hands in hers.

"What is it?" she asked. "Whatever it is, I'm right by yer side."

He looked at her then with such feeling, Anne knew that this, whatever it was, had been sent to bring them back closer together.

"Do yer promise me that, lass?" he asked. "It's a bad business, worse than..."

"I promise, Joseph. I'm yer wife."

*

The fire moved and cracked while he spoke. There were moments, then, when she wanted to block him out and let the

17

fire take over. There were moments when she felt the thud of his words inside her head and the burn of the flames near her skin and she thought she would never move again.

"Dead?" she repeated. "Are yer sure she's dead?"

"Of course I'm sure, woman," he snapped. "Don't yer think I would have made damn sure before I put 'er in the ground?"

He saw her smart and her expression flinch slightly and he tried to calm himself. Shouting would do no good. Getting angry with her now wouldn't help him at all. He needed her on side more than ever.

"Oh, Joseph," Anne wailed. "Oh, Joseph."

"'Ere," he said. "It were an accident. I din't mean to. It were dark and she were..."

Anne looked at him in the dimly lit room. It was something in the way he said she. There was the faintest hint of affection, or at least intimacy.

"It were 'er, weren't it?" she asked. "She's the reason yer don't look at me. It were 'er yer were with all these times yer din't come 'ome when yer should 'ave." She could hear her voice coming out bolder, stronger, like it had been held down so long and now it rose. "Oh, Joseph, she were no more than a bairn."

"She were seventeen! And she had the devil in 'er!" he shouted. He stood up now and turned around. Bess got to her feet and looked up at him, wagging her tail. He turned back to face his wife. She was sitting very still, looking up at him and waiting. "See, Anne," he went on. "I'd bin in t' Low Drop, and... I don't know, there were somert. They knew. They knew all about it."

"What are yer saying, Joseph?" she asked. "They knew she were dead? 'Ow could they?"

"No, no, yer not listening, woman." He saw her face sting again, retract as if he'd threatened to slap her. He brought the softness back. He needed her. He fell to his knees in front of her and took her hands in his. "They knew about me and Sarah," he said. "I know they did. Mr Vernon's neighbour were there, and they near on told me to leave."

"Are yer sure?"

"Sure as I can be. And there's somert else."

Anne could feel his warm hands encasing hers. She couldn't remember the last time she'd felt that. She rubbed her thumb against the insides of his fingers and looked into his eyes. "What is it?" she asked.

"When I were... burying 'er, I swear there were someone watching. Only, I din't see 'em properly. It were more of a feeling. I could feel I were being watched. I could feel there were someone there. And then when I turned around I just saw this shadow move. Quick. It moved off quick. Bess were barking, and I went to t' edge o' t' trees, but there were no one there. Still. Someone saw me, Anne, I'm sure someone saw me."

*

When Anne walked away from the house the next morning she was sure of where she should go and what she should do.

Joseph had been up and at the land early, even earlier than usual. So early, the murk and cling of darkness must have been close on his clothes and his hands when he bent and pulled, when he stretched and broke the land, heaved and carried and worked the earth. He'd been up and out of the house too early for talking. Anne had stirred as he washed and dressed, Bess's paws skitting on the floorboards, her tail beating the doorframe as it wagged while she passed from room to room behind Joseph.

Anne had closed her eyes against the sounds. The memory of the night before and all the things he'd said brought a sickness into her stomach and a buzzing to her head. She'd experienced that short blissful moment on waking when she'd forgotten it all. Then it leapt back at her and made her mind struggle in the tangle of it.

Anne went about the cold house that morning with a strange feeling working inside her. What Joseph had told her last night was terrible. It was worse than she could ever have imagined. And yet, amidst the worry and the dread and the terrible sadness of it all, Anne could feel something like excitement turn in her chest. What Joseph had done was unforgivable, but it did give Anne a slow blinking idea of hope. It was a bad business alright. But it was something. At least it was something.

She closed the heavy door behind her and left the house. The snow was light today, flitting in the air like the scattered heads of dandelions in summer. It fell softly onto her face and left cold streaks like tears on her skin. As she pulled away from the house she began to feel exposed. She walked from the path and felt a fuzz on her left cheek, a secret she now held tickling her flesh. The woods up to the right, behind the house, lit the outside corner of her eye. She thought of worms round a body. Heavy damp earth creeping into eyes and mouth and ears.

She walked quickly away, into the lane, the swell of the land on the horizon on the other side of the village, the dip down to the houses and the church before her. She left her home behind her and she walked out into the morning, her feet slipping on the icy path, the cold melted snow seeping through her shoes already.

"Morning, Mrs Bradshaw."

Anne looked up and saw the woman who lived in one of the cottages by the stream. She walked slowly down the lane, watching Anne in a stern kind of way. Anne lifted her head at the woman, but found no words to speak.

The air seemed to get colder as she walked down the hill, as if the trees up by the house had sheltered her and protected her from the swirling winter wind. She kept her head down, her chin pushing against her chest, and she walked the bend and dip of the lane. Once in the village, she came to the church and slowed a little, gazing up at the tower, solid and dependable against the smoke-grey sky. Two more women from the village were passing by the gate which led to the path of the church, their heads bent against the biting air, their bodies close to each other for warmth, huddled as they walked.

"I heard it from Mrs Turner," one of them said. "Mr Vernon's in a terrible way over it. And George, of course."

The other woman tutted and shook her head. "That

poor man'll find no peace on this earth, the Lord taking his wife like that, and now..."

Just then the two women noticed Anne standing there. They paused and seemed frozen like the air and the ground beneath them for a moment. Anne thought she even saw one of them blush.

"Mrs Bradshaw," said the one who had tutted and shook her head. "We were just talking about poor Mr Vernon. You know 'is Sarah din't come 'ome last night and no one's an idea where she is."

The words were held, passed from the woman's dry lips and into the space between herself and Anne. Anne stared at the woman who had spoken, the weight of all she said heavy on all their faces. Anne could feel her skin freezing and becoming paler, her breathing hot in the air in front of her face, her heart rattling and her hands beginning to shake.

"Excuse me," she murmured. And she pushed past the women, opened the creaking church gate and hurried down the path.

*

The church was quiet except for an occasional boom of noise from outside which found its way in through cracks in windows or holes in the corners, and echoed around the cold stone building. A call from someone to another, heavy work in the nearby fields.

Anne walked slowly up the aisle, remembering, like a splinter in skin, her wedding day. When she had smiled shyly beneath her veil and clutched her father's arm as he led her sternly to meet her new husband at the front of the church. All that seemed so long ago now. Though it wasn't. It wasn't that long at all. Just a few slowly-shaded years.

Anne's father had been happy with the match. He said Joseph was a hard-working God-fearing man, and a farmer like him. Alright, so Joseph wasn't educated. He couldn't read and write, even a little, like Anne could. But that wasn't his fault, Anne's father reasoned. Not every child was lucky enough to be shown the ways of reading and writing at home like Anne had been. Maybe Joseph's parents weren't so devout. Perhaps they felt it was enough for Joseph to attend church and listen to the word of God without reading it for himself. Anne's father might not agree with that viewpoint, but it wasn't Joseph's fault. Couldn't blame the lad for that. And in every other way, so far as Anne's father could see, Joseph was an ideal husband for his daughter. Devoted to the land, serious, he understood the way of things, Anne's father said. He would provide.

But he hadn't provided the one thing Anne wanted most. Not yet. Although, if she mentioned it, Joseph would get angry and say it was Anne's fault. Some problem with her body. Something she was or wasn't doing.

"That's women's stuff," he'd say. "No use lookin' to me for that, lass, it'll 'appen when it 'appens and not before if you don't have the makin' for it."

Anne knew now, better than ever, that wasn't the case. She may not be particularly educated or experienced in these matters, but even Anne knew there was something which had to be done in order for children to come along. And Joseph had not been doing that with Anne for some time. He'd been doing that with Sarah Vernon.

Anne approached a pew and put her hand out to steady herself. The thought of her husband with that she-devil... Joseph had said it himself: Sarah had darkness in her. To think, for a brief hooded moment last night, Anne had felt pity for the girl.

She edged her way into the pew and bent her head. Maybe it was a blessing. Maybe this bad business had a light shining right through it. All part of the Lord's plan. Or even, perhaps, Joseph had done a good thing last night. The girl was almost certainly evil.

Anne closed her eyes and breathed deeply. She could feel the clammy wetness from the snow on the ground outside invading her shoes still and bothering her feet. She clasped her hands together and held her fingers over-tightly. The Lord would surely look kindly on them. Joseph had not acted out of malice. It was an accident, like he'd said, and, anyway, after all, Sarah Vernon was carrying the devil inside her.

Anne opened her eyes again and looked up. She had heard the quick soft lift and fall of feet approaching. The pastor came forward from the vestry and walked quickly towards the back of the church. He smiled at Anne as he passed, but his eyes held a weight of knowledge and suspicion, pulled by sadness, that made something old turn over in Anne's middle.

She'd come here to gain some peace of mind. She'd come for a sign, some affirmation, that she was right. This was where she knew she would find the answers. Here, in this building. This was where she would feel it. And, she told herself, no matter how anyone looked at her or what anyone said under their muttering breaths, she did feel it. What she was doing was right.

She got up to leave the church, and the door behind her opened. A fast wind blew in with specks of snow, first lifting Anne's hair a little and then moving forward to the big bible open at the altar. The freezing wind, softened by its journey forward inside the church, ruffled the pages of the bible, making them leap like desire. Then it seemed to leave. Anne looked quickly in the direction of the open door. The pastor was putting a hand to a man's shoulder. The man's head bent as he shuffled inside the church. Anne could still feel the cold fingers of the wind in her hair, only a moment ago. And something even colder in her shoulders and down her back. The pastor was talking in low soothing tones as the man made his way inside. They were about to close the door again when the pastor looked up at Anne, a warning in his eyes. She made her feet move and she rushed to the door before it could close. Only then did Mr Vernon look up from his misery and see her. She locked eyes with him for the briefest second but she couldn't detect any anger, only the deep clawing of sadness.

*

Out in the cold morning light, the sky like muddied ice, Anne stood for a moment, leaning her body against the stone church wall. She put her hand to her chest and felt her heart rocking. She closed her eyes and tried to tame her breathing. He had looked her in the face. Mr Vernon. Sarah's father. He must have seen the guilt wriggling in her skin. But how could he know? How could any of them know? The woman in the lane, the two by the church gate, the pastor.

Anne forced herself to stand up straight and, still clutching her chest, she walked up the path and away from the church.

Maybe it was her imagination. Maybe none of them knew or suspected anything, and it was only Anne's state of mind playing these cruel tricks. She calmed herself enough to open the gate at the top of the graveyard and step out into the lane again. Her feet slid a little on the smoothed-over ice at the edges of the path. Her hand grasped the wall and she stopped and took a deep breath. There was no one in the lane. She stood and glanced down the street to see if anyone was coming her way, then up to where she would walk, making sure she'd meet no one whose face she would have to acknowledge and hide from. But she was safe. There was no one.

She looked down at the ice-covered snow on the ground where her feet slipped. The snow had only fallen in light sugar-like flurries so far that morning. It was lost on the ice, but in between, where the path was worn by so many boots and the snow was melted away, Anne could see the tiny flakes like innocent little footprints. Each one was melting soon after it lay. Alive for the briefest moment and then gone.

She put her hand to her belly. The need for a child was in every turn of her eyes. It overwhelmed her and made everything else in the world insignificant. Her love for Joseph, she thought to herself, was the same. These people around her in the village didn't know anything. Perhaps they thought they did, but they didn't know. Sarah Vernon only had herself to blame for what happened. Besides, no one could prove a thing.

Anne took the sharp morning air into her lungs and breathed slowly. Everything would be fine. She stepped out into the lane and began walking back up the road. It was quiet now. A few birds shimmied in the air and sailed down onto bushes by the side of the road. Anne saw a robin sitting quietly in the tight branches of a tree. She smiled and walked on. She would soothe Joseph and take him to her bed tonight. She would create a new life for them both to focus on and they would forget all about this bad business.

Anne was thinking about the fire she would light later tonight for when Joseph came home, the food she would prepare, the ale she would pour for him, the way she would persuade him back into her arms, when she rounded the corner and saw something strange.

Up ahead, where the road bent around and the lane dipped, Anne saw someone flit from one side of the road to the other. It was someone. And yet... she couldn't tell who it was. Not even if it was a man or a woman or a boy or a girl. It was just a shape. Just the shape of someone moving quickly from path to path. The dip in the lane hid the whole of the form from her view and Anne stopped dead and peered ahead at where the person had moved. It was as if they had left a shadow in the air, a fresh memory of themselves in the cold space where they had just been. It was as if they were fluid.

Anne knew who it was. There was only one person it could be.

Snow began to thicken and fall from weighty dark clouds that rumbled forward. Anne moved slowly, still peering at the dip in the lane where the figure had been, but they were gone, and the snow covered the view like a swarm of bees.

Today

Glenn always took Lorraine to the same hotel. The cheap one in town. Whenever they walked in together Lorraine saw a glance of recognition lift in the receptionist's eyes. Of course she knew. She probably saw this kind of thing going on all the time. Why should she care? As long as they were paying for their room and drinks in the bar, why would anyone care?

It was only a cheap hotel, but Lorraine didn't mind. She liked the homely feel to the bar, the way the barman watched them as they sat close together and kissed and drank gin and stroked each other's legs. She liked the warmth of the blue-and-cream carpet that ran the staircase, the pictures of stately homes on the walls. She even liked the poor beds, tucked under with thin sheets and topped with uneven pillows, and the TV that never worked properly. Not that she and Glenn ever watched TV. Not that they had time for that. They would always drop into the room and get straight to it. Always. Glenn was like a dog, always hungry. Lorraine had heard once that if you put a week's worth of food down for a dog it would eat the lot in one go, didn't know how to pace itself, didn't understand when it was full. Glenn was like that.

She glanced at him now as he swung the car away from town, up to the right.

"Where are we going?" she asked.

She saw his mouth twitch a little, an uncertain feeling enter his features through his skin.

"Hotel," he said.

"Hotel's in town. Where are we going?"

"Different hotel."

She stared at him while he drove. She didn't like it when something changed, not without her knowing first, not without her being in on the game and why they were playing.

"What different hotel?" she asked. "Why?"

He shrugged. "Just thought..."

She smiled, but she couldn't, and didn't want to, hide her annoyance. "Don't give me that. You didn't just think anything. Why are we going to a different hotel? We always

26

go to the same hotel."

"This one's nicer."

"Just tell me, Glenn."

He glanced at her quickly then back to the road. Her black hair looked like nylon in this light. Coarse and dead against the cold sleet-filled sky. She dyed it too much. Probably straightened it and blew it dry and tortured it until it was no longer the thing it had once been. He glanced at her again. She was still staring at him, still waiting for an answer she could believe.

"Alright," he said. "Staff in the usual place were getting a bit too... familiar. I don't want everyone knowing my business and I just felt they were" – he shrugged again – "nosy."

"What do you mean, nosy?"

"Aw, you know, looking at us in that way, little remarks, those knowing smiles."

She grinned. "I thought you liked all that. Thought it turned you on, the danger."

But he didn't smile back. "Yeah well, not when they've got my name and address and credit card details and everything. I've got a lot to lose, Lorraine, you know that. Anybody starts talking and it gets out, I'm the one with everything to lose."

Derbyshire, 1760s

Back inside the dim little hovel, away from the snow and the
wind on the road, Aaron sat by his mother. The old woman
seemed to sleep more and more these last few days and the
fire Aaron kept alight, and tended to like it was a baby, didn't
keep her warm anymore. She was quiet. Aaron's mother had
never been quiet, as far as he knew. She was always talking.
Always telling him about his father, who Aaron couldn't
remember, and her mother before her, who had been like her,
and her mother before that, and on and on. Now she just
complained of the cold. Aaron did his best to keep her warm
with what little they had, but her old voice would creep out
slow and heavy like cattle in summer. "Cold, Aaron, lad.
'Ere." And she would gesture with her arm for him to
approach her again. "Must be a bad winter, lad, is it?"

"Yes, mother," he would say, almost to humour her.
Then he would pull the blankets tighter around her legs and
her shawl closer around her chest and he would listen as she
told him again how to ease her suffering and smooth her way.

Aaron's mother spoke the names of nature he needed
to go out and collect, and waved her hand in the direction of
the saved dried bundles she still had. "Just a little," she said,
and she made a pinching dropping motion with her branch-
like hand. "Though you know this," she said. "I told you."

Aaron wanted to see his mother up on her feet, poking
the fire with her stick and laughing at the gossip from the
village, but he knew that if she passed this winter she wouldn't
pass another, and he wouldn't see her how she'd been before
ever again. He knelt on the cold ground and looked around the
room. People still came to the door now and then. They still
walked up from the village and cut away where the road
dipped, walked down between the trees, their feet slipping on
smoothed stones and ice, and announced themselves at the
hovel Aaron lived in with his mother. People still came,
wanting help, treatment, a cure, or just an easing of their
troubled minds. Aaron knew he had to deal with these people
by himself now.

He tried to imagine what it would be like when his mother had passed. When it would be just him. Alone in this place. Knowledge like the shifting sky. Like heavy full clouds. It was difficult sometimes, this life. It was hard sometimes to keep everything separate. Only yesterday evening he'd had a man at the door with questions riddling his mind, worry clinging in his chest and desire laying in his organ. The man, a widower, was made a mouse by his love for his neighbour's daughter. He stood inside the hovel with Aaron and near on begged him to help him. Change the way her eyes set when she saw him. Cast a spell. Make her want him. Do something.

"I know yer can," the man had said.

Aaron had stood quiet for a moment. He thought hard, his brain tagging the things he knew and working them into words he could speak. He told the man it wasn't as simple as that.

"No one can alter the course of another's heart," he said. "I could only bring out the love she already feels..." Aaron paused. He put his fingers to his bearded face and held them there for a moment, his gaze resting on the ground. Then he looked up, straight into the man's eyes. "In your case, sir," he said, "this would not be helpful to you. The woman you speak of loves another. I know this to be true."

"'Ow do yer know this?" the man asked.

"She goes to him when darkness comes upon the day," he went on. Then he tapped his own head. "I have seen it."

The speed with which the man caught hold of Aaron then, his anger flooding his face and his fists tight around the fabric of Aaron's clothes, was so alarming Aaron thought he might cry out.

"Who is it?" the man demanded. "Tell me! Who does she go to?"

Aaron tried to shush the man. His fury was so shocking, Aaron could feel himself tremble. He said in whispers that his mother was sleeping in her chair behind them and Aaron didn't want to cause her any disturbance. But the man's anger was high in his blood and he didn't let go of Aaron.

"Tell me!" he shouted.

Aaron knew he had never been a brave man. He had lived a solitary life with his mother and had never before faced anything quite like this. He wasn't brave but, still, the ease with which he spoke the name of Joseph was a surprise even to himself.

*

He knelt up on the floor now and looked at his mother. He was not at all sure he could carry this life off. Much of his time, when he wasn't walking or gathering the plants he needed to bring home, he spent making things from wood, carving bowls and figures and other trinkets. He was good at it, and he wondered if he should just follow that path and leave this other one. But he didn't see as he had much choice. His mother had spent her life teaching him, and the people who lived around here expected him to do this. She had suggested to him that he could combine the two. She had shown him the symbols he should carve into cleaned shaped wood to influence the minds of the villagers. She had shown him with her stick in the dry flaky earth which symbols would have what effect. Aaron did as his mother showed him, as she told him, as he always did. Though it still wasn't his choice.

He crouched by his mother and watched her breathing, tightened the shawl around her chest and laid his head close to her shoulder.

She stirred. "Must be a bad winter, lad, is it?" she said.

Aaron thought about the woman, Mrs Bradshaw, walking up the path today, the snow covering her as she slowed and saw him. He thought about the night he'd seen the woman's husband, Joseph, among the trees with Sarah Vernon, first alive, pushed hard against the bark, Aaron drifting up on the horizon with the cattle and the low moon. Him coming back here to find Sarah's neighbour, George, sick with love for her. Then Joseph Bradshaw, taking Sarah limp and lifeless in his arms and digging her shallow grave. Aaron had heard the dog snarl and the shovel hit the frozen ground again and again. He'd watched from below for a moment, then he'd turned and run.

"Aye, that it is, mother," he answered. "It's a bad winter."

Today

The hotel was miles away from anywhere. Glenn pulled into the car park and drove carefully on the icy gravel and into a space.

"See," he said. "Much better than that other old dump."

Lorraine sat forward in the car and looked up at the hotel. It was old. Really old. Lorraine had never been any good at history at school or anything, but even she could see this building was really old.

"Well, yeah," she said. "We're really staying here?"

Glenn relaxed, smiled at her and put his hand firmly on her knee. "Only the best for you," he said. "Come on."

They took their overnight bags and went into the hotel. Even the door seemed old, and when Glenn checked in at the desk the receptionist presented him with an actual key. Lorraine stood beside him and stared at the large key as the woman behind the desk spoke about breakfast and room service. This must be a really old place, she thought. Nowhere uses actual keys anymore.

Glenn was opening his wallet and sliding his credit card out. The receptionist glanced at Lorraine once and Lorraine felt the same suspicion fall as always. The same look drifting in the receptionist's eyes. Why would a man like Glenn be spending a night in a hotel with a woman like Lorraine? Pretty obvious really, Lorraine thought. Not that she was bothered. Not that she cared. She wandered away from Glenn's side and began peering at the photos on the walls. These old places probably always had old photos up like this, she thought. Just to reinforce the point. Just in case you were in any doubt. It's old. Has photos to prove it. Can charge double for the privilege. Probably costs a fortune, she thought. Not that she cared. Glenn always paid. She wouldn't be here if he didn't.

She glanced back over at the receptionist for a moment. Small mousy woman. She was probably jealous, that was probably why she'd looked at Lorraine like that. She probably couldn't get a set-up like this if she tried. She probably saw Lorraine's long black hair and even tan and tight top and wished she looked this good.

She caught the woman's eye and turned quickly back to the photos on the wall. One of the hotel from about a million years ago, Lorraine thought. Really old. Some bloke with a horse standing outside it. Then one of a village Lorraine guessed must be round here somewhere, though she didn't know it. She moved along the wall, peering at the pictures. She had an odd sense of something coming, something building. The next few pictures weren't photos but sketches. Must be of the place from way back then, she thought. Before photos. Although they could just be whatsit – artists impressions or whatever. She peered at the pictures. The hotel again. Didn't look like it did today. Looked sort of... lopsided. The roof was bowed in the middle and the people standing around outside it looked like they were dressed in cloaks or something. Next one was the village again. Sketched in pencil or something. Lorraine stared harder at this one. It showed a house with some figures in the foreground and a wood behind it. The picture was a simple drawing, but the edges were so shaded and the building so darkened with lead it was as if the whole picture was covered in soot. The sky held a few rumbling clouds and the windows of the house were all black. Lorraine leaned forward. There was a small crowd gathered around in front of the house and one lone tall figure, holding something in his hands up in the air in front of him like a chalice or a sacrifice or something... something important.

"Lorraine."

Glenn touched her shoulder and she jumped. "Oh shit, Glenn, you scared me to death!"

He laughed a little. "Bit jumpy, aren't you?" he said. "You know what you need." And he waved the key in front of her face. "Come on, sexy."

*

An hour later Lorraine lay on the bed reading the room service menu. Glenn came out of the bathroom and threw himself down next to her.

"What do you fancy?" he asked.

She didn't look up, just carried on scanning the menu. "I don't know," she said. "What do you fancy?"

He ran his fingers up the side of her bare back. "You," he said.

Lorraine peered at him from the corner of her eye. They didn't usually talk much like that. "Oh yeah?" she said.

"Yeah, course I do, you know I do."

"What did you get me, then?" she asked.

He got up from the bed and went over to his overnight bag. Unzipped it and brought out a package. She hauled herself up onto her elbows to open the gift. Inside she found a platinum necklace with a single ruby drop. She gazed at it and took it in her fingers. It was beautiful. Lorraine imagined Glenn would buy an amazing engagement ring. Though Lorraine would never find out. Lorraine already had one of those, and the wedding ring to match. Neither of which were particularly amazing. But Lorraine's husband was docile and tolerant and very forgiving. And he worked away a lot. That suited Lorraine.

She rolled the necklace in her fingers. "I like that!" she said.

Glenn lay down next to her again. "Glad you like it," he said. He paused for a moment. Lorraine looked at him. He was going to say something. Something serious. She braced herself and waited.

"You know, I..."

"Glenn."

"No, no, don't worry, I wasn't going to... Just, you know, how I feel about you, but, you know..."

She eyed him warily. "Go on," she said.

"Well, you know I can never leave Julia."

She looked back at the necklace in her hand. "I know," she said.

"Because I can't afford to, not because I don't want to, you know, I'd lose the business, she'd take me for all I've got..."

"Glenn, you don't have to say anything, really, it's

fine."

Lorraine felt the discomfort hold her closely for a few minutes. She continued turning the necklace in her fingers, the ruby rolling over and sparkling where the light from above hit it hard. There was a silence between them. Somewhere deep in the silence Lorraine began to think.

Derbyshire, 1760s

Aaron could see, in the dim room, his mother's eyes closing again.

"Mother," he whispered. But she didn't reply. He put his palm to her chest and felt her breathing. It seemed slight, like an easy breeze, but tangled by some ailment. Aaron didn't know how much longer she would live.

"Mother," he said. "What would you do if you knew something, if you'd seen something bad? Would you tell?"

He waited, the slow rhythmic breathing of his old mother filling the room. He thought she wouldn't answer, that she was asleep, or worse. He sunk down on his knees and thought again about how he would manage on his own. Aaron didn't feel wise enough for all this. What would he do when he no longer had his mother to guide him?

He looked up at her crooked face, her sunken cheeks and her weather worn skin, her hair like a sleet-filled sky, wild by the sides of her face. She didn't open her eyes again, just said, "See all and say nowt, lad."

A Bad Winter

Today

Lorraine always slept well when she was with Glenn. She put it down to the fact that she didn't care. Why should she? If she ever said the next morning that she'd had the best sleep, that she always slept like the dead when she was with Glenn, he'd say, "That's 'cause I wear you out, gorgeous." Or something like that. And she'd smile. She really did like it when he said things like that. She really did. But it was just a game.

She turned over in the bed. He was asleep already. She could sense the calming rise and fall of his breathing. He didn't snore, not like her husband, but he always turned away from her in the bed... not like her husband. Lorraine's husband was the affectionate type. Not Glenn's kind of affection. Not sex mad. But the loving kind of affection. Lorraine's husband was all cuddles and holding hands. She supposed she should be happy with that. But she wasn't. He didn't satisfy her. But then no man did.

She shifted in the bed. Glenn was a heavy sleeper. Not like Lorraine. There could be a fight going on right there in the room and he wouldn't wake. But he was alright. She shouldn't complain. She took what she could, she took the parts and pieces of the men she found and she fitted them into her. If only there was a man who was made up of all these things, she thought. If only there was someone who could be all that she wanted.

She stared into the dark room. If she had a man like that, would she be happy? Would she?

The lights from a passing car swept over the room for the briefest moment. Lorraine lay with her eyes open, staring around at the sofa and the dressing table and the free-standing mirror. She was thinking about how complicated her life had become, but she didn't feel any guilt, not really. Maybe a fleeting moment of it. Maybe now and then, but not enough to trouble her. She was thinking how she didn't even mind this when another car passed and the lights flashed into the room fast. It was only a second, probably not even that, but as the lights hit the free-standing mirror, Lorraine saw a woman. She heard a sound escape her own mouth, though she hadn't meant to make it, and then she was burrowing into Glenn's back, holding her arms around him and shouting at him to wake up.

*

He turned over, his bulky torso rolling as her arms stretched around him. She still had her face shoved into his skin.

"What the bloody hell?" he said.

"In the mirror! I saw something in the mirror!"

"What are you talking about?"

He was sitting up now, reaching for the light next to the bed and running his hand over his sleep-filled face.

Lorraine stayed lying down in the bed, clinging onto his body. As the light blinked into the room she cautiously looked behind her.

"I saw it, Glenn," she said. "I wasn't dreaming, I wasn't asleep, I really saw it."

"What? What did you see?"

"A woman. Right there!" She pointed behind her at the mirror.

Glenn peered over at the free-standing mirror. "Well, that would just be a reflection of something. What's wrong with you? First you were all jumpy down in reception and now this! Didn't think you were the type to get all hysterical over something so silly."

"It wasn't a reflection! A car went past and the headlights in the room... and... and I saw it!"

"What are you saying? You think you saw a *ghost*?"

He said the word with such force. Like it was stupid. Like it was feeble. She hesitated. Began to sit up in the bed. He was right. It wasn't like her. But she did see it.

"Well... I don't know," she said. "I definitely saw something, someone."

Glenn sighed. She could tell he just wanted to go back to sleep. Didn't care what she'd seen. "It's dark, babe," he said. "It's an old building and it's late." He was stroking her hair now, bringing her head into his shoulder. "You just saw a reflection of something in the room, that's all."

38

Lorraine could feel her whole body begin to calm. "You think so?" she asked.

"I know it," he answered. He coaxed her back down into the bed and he reached over to turn out the light.

Just then, a pure second ago, Glenn had stroked her hair and cradled her head with... affection. Wasn't it? It was definitely something like that. It certainly felt like that. Whatever it was, it had calmed her instantly. It made her feel better, safer.

"Hold me," she said.

"Hold you?"

"Yes. Please."

"You're being silly, Lorraine, but... OK."

He put his arms around her and lay her head on his chest. Lorraine didn't know how it felt to Glenn, but to her it felt like something she'd never had but had always missed. The rise and fall of his chest was almost rocking her to sleep. She caught herself just before she dropped off and sleep took her under. Don't go getting silly, she told herself. Watch yourself. Don't go getting any daft ideas, now.

*

The light came through like the sea. She was aware of it as she moved. Something huge and uncompromising. Above her. All around her. But the trees made its movement difficult. The trees were closer to her, their branches bending over her head like arms in a childhood game or a dance, arching over for her to pass underneath. The light was the important thing, though. She felt it.

She moved around the thin trunks of trees, looking up and watching the sky travel beneath the fingers of branches like water between boats. She wasn't naked. But she wasn't aware of what she wore either.

It was the strangest feeling.

She thought the wood might go on forever, her moving in it like this forever, but then the trees cleared a little and a dog barked soundlessly in front of her. She stared at the dog as it stood hunched backwards against her, teeth bared, ears back, barking with no voice.

The scene was upon her quickly, before she had time to prepare. The man was there, bent slightly, spade thrusting into the ground, sweat on his skin, something low and quiet in his eyes. He looked at her. She knew him. Somehow she knew him. But her gaze fell to the ground where his spade dug. There she saw the half-covered face of a girl, sky-white skin, orange leaves wet on her cheek, dark earth speckled around her still eyes.

*

There was a sound. Lorraine felt it bring her out like a fast wind in a tunnel. At that moment when she woke up she could still hear it. She wasn't dreaming; she would tell Glenn when she forced him from sleep again. It was the sound that woke her up, she didn't dream it.

She'd been shaking him, his torso shifting in the bed while her hand roughly moved him.

"Glenn," she hissed. "Glenn! Wake up! Did you hear that?"

He rolled over to face her, his fingers about his face, displacing sleep in his skin. "What the fuck?"

"Did you hear it?"

"Hear what?"

"That noise. It woke me up. Didn't you hear it?"

"No, I didn't fucking hear it, but you've woken me up."

Lorraine looked cautiously around the room. She hardly dared to look at the mirror, but when she did she saw the morning light coming through the curtains and reflecting the whole of the room in the glass. That was it. Nothing else.

Glenn was sitting up in the bed, rubbing his hand over his face and head. He turned to her, his hand held cupped in front of his face now like anger waiting, or tenderness – she couldn't tell.

"What's got into you?" he asked. "You've been a mess since we got here. What's going on?"

"Nothing's going on," she said. "Except this place. It's not me, it's this room, or this hotel, I don't know."

She sat up to meet his body. She took his hand from where it hovered near his face and held his fingers in hers. "Didn't you hear it?" she asked.

He looked at her sharply. "Hear what?"

"That noise. Like a thudding noise, like something heavy. It woke me up, and I was having this weird dream."

"What weird dream?"

"I was in the woods or something and this man was... digging, and there was this dead girl, and then that noise woke me up."

When she looked at him, Glenn was frowning at her. "Jesus, Lorraine. What's going on with you?"

"I told you, nothing! It's this place."

"Oh yeah? Well then how come I didn't see anything or hear anything?"

They sat and looked at each other for a moment. It seemed strange then, just for a second, to be sitting so physically close to someone and yet be so far apart.

She dismissed his look. "You'd sleep through anything, you know you would," she said.

"And the dream?"

"What about it?"

He pulled her towards him with her hands. The irritation had all but left his body now and his voice was lower, and soft like the sheets around her. She knew what he was doing. She knew he wanted to end this conversation and lie back down in the bed with her. "You had a bad dream," he said. "And the noise was either in the dream or..."

"It wasn't a bad dream, it was just weird, and the noise wasn't in the dream, it woke me up."

"...or you heard something coming from another room. We are in a hotel, after all. All kinds of things go on in hotel rooms. You know that. Could have been anything." He leaned forward and began kissing her neck. She was still frowning, but she already knew she soon wouldn't be. She resisted slightly, pulling away, but Glenn persisted and Lorraine could feel her annoyance with him sliding.

"Maybe someone was at it all night," he said. "Maybe

someone was having an even dirtier night away than us."

He was such a dog. But he got her with it every time. Lorraine could feel her body relax into him, and the memory of the dream and what she'd thought she'd seen in the mirror – what was surely just her imagination or a reflection, just like Glenn said – go dull and start to fall away. She could feel herself becoming calmer, the smile spreading across her face. "We can soon sort that out," she said.

Derbyshire, 1760s

In the house, as the sky grew dark outside and made shadows deepen in the corners of the rooms, Anne went about her business. Sweeping the floor and boiling water, scrubbing clothes and baking bread, occupying her hands and hoping her mind would follow them. Anne's mind was likely to wander today. She steered it as best she could away from the lifeless Sarah buried between the trees and back to Joseph. The thought of Joseph being with her as he once had been filled Anne with a joy she hadn't felt in some time. It was worth the bad thoughts. It was worth anything.

When Joseph came in he washed without a word and sat down for his meal. Anne looked at him as he ate. He'd picked up the old sword he kept by the fire on his way through the house and he sat with it on the table now, playing with its blade and turning it over in his palms while he ate with his other hand. It was a short sword, only the length of his forearm, and he handled it easily like it was part of him. Anne watched him. There were no words she could find in her that would soften his face and relieve his worry. He kept his gaze down on his food and he ate quickly. When he had finished he stretched his arms and then, bringing his hands back down on to the table, said, "This sword was in my family... It's somert real, somert yer can touch. All I 'ave from my family." He put his hand through the metal handle and held the sword as it was meant to be held. "I shan't be going t' t' Low Drop," he said.

"No," she answered carefully. "For a day or two, perhaps."

"Aye, for a day or two."

Anne got to her feet to clear away the things from the table. She noticed from the corner of her eye Joseph flexing his fingers on the table top and holding the sword firmly with his other hand.

"Leave that, lass," he said.

Anne had her back to him now and turned slightly to see him still sitting there. He suddenly looked stronger than she remembered, broader, his skin rougher, and his hair,

43

which covered most of his body, darker.

"It won't take a minute," she said.

She heard the scrape of the chair on the stone floor as he pushed it back and got to his feet. "I said leave it," he answered.

She felt his arms tight around her middle and his body pressing her forward where she stood. He still held the sword, but now he held it close to Anne's chest, the blade like wire against her. She tried to speak but the sound that escaped her, as Joseph pressed her further, was more of a grunt. His free hand was fast up inside her clothes, pulling them until his fingers found her flesh. Then he turned her around and pushed her forward over the table, the sword cold against the skin of her neck. When her husband entered her then, Anne thought about the man her mother had described to her before her wedding. And Anne thought that her mother had been wrong about him. Joseph didn't become this man when he'd taken a drink. He became this man when he had no place and no other person to let it out to.

*

Anne stayed by the table for some time after. Joseph fed the fire and stared into it, the sword propped back up by its side. Then he moved suddenly, as if his body followed as soon as he had the thought, and he whistled fast and Bess got to her feet where she sat, her ears up, her legs ready.

Anne thought it was only once Joseph had left the house to walk with Bess that she breathed again.

*

Joseph couldn't walk the woods. He looked to where the trees stood against the sky like bars at a window and he felt a pain in his chest that seemed like it would stop his breath. He couldn't go anywhere near that place. Not yet. The thought of Sarah being in the earth up there. The idea of stepping on the ground that covered her. He could hardly bear it. He turned his face away from the trees and walked into the lane. It was dark now and the snow dripped from the clouds. The freezing air was beginning to break. Joseph was sure. In a few days the air

44

would warm a little and the ice on the ground would begin to melt. Work would be easier then and he could spend more time out at the land. Eventually the days would lighten and become longer.

He walked in the lane with Bess trotting beside him. There was no one about and, even if there had been, in this light and with this weather, they'd have a job on knowing him. He imagined what he would do if Mr Vernon or his mad neighbour came upon him now. It struck him, then, that this would be a difficult business. Not just right now but at any time. He tried to figure a future but found it more clouded than the winter sky. He tried to think of a time when he could visit Sarah's grave between the trees but the thought became too complicated and he let it hang.

He and Bess had walked the lane, into the dip in the road and out again until they stopped at the head of the village, where the street ran down from the hill he stood on. The dark sky rumbled behind him and Bess waited and looked up at his still face. The snow was lighter, falling like flour, and down in the village Joseph could see the light from the Low Drop. The sign that hung outside, "The Kingston Arms", squeaked as it swayed in the cold wind. Joseph fancied that, inside, the men would be laughing and drinking by the fire. Or talking in low voices about trouble, about him, maybe, about Sarah missing. He thought that in a few days it would all settle, like the soft snow, and then melt away. People would forget and leave it behind. Then Joseph would walk back down the hill and into the Low Drop.

He turned slowly on the hill now, Bess following his body and turning with him, and walked back towards the house.

*

In the Kingston Arms the fire cracked and beer was poured. The landlord stretched out his hands on the bar and listened to the talk between the men. He put a word to the conversation here and there, but mostly he listened.

"I'm telling you!" George shouted. "'E's behind this."

Another man sat forward and leaned with his jug on

the table. "'Appen you're right about 'im and Sarah, though I don't even put much by that, but 'appen it's true..." He paused and glanced around him. "Yer can't rightly blame the man for that." He shrugged. "Joseph Bradshaw's a decent sort, is all I'm saying."

"A decent sort? 'E's been 'aving his way with Sarah while 'is wife sits indoors. Call that a decent sort?"

The other man leaned back, taking his jug from the table and raising it to his face. "It's nothing tha wouldn't 'ave done thiself if tha'd 'ad chance," he said. "That's what tha's getting so upset about."

A round of laughter travelled the room.

"And you 'er father's neighbour and old enough to be 'er father!"

George stamped his jug down on the table. "I'm telling you!" he shouted. "'E's seen to 'er." He leaned forward and stared at the man, then addressed the others sitting around him. "I 'eard it first from old Mattson's son, them that live up by t' stream. 'E told me, and 'e knows, 'e sees things, don't none of yer tell me yer don't know it's true. 'Is old mother cured your missus!" He pointed to a man sitting to his right and the man nodded.

"Aye, that she did."

"And others of yer 'ere," George went on. "You know it. And it was 'im that told me. 'E saw it. Bradshaw and Sarah, and now she's missing."

The room went quiet. The landlord watched on and listened, and even the man sitting at the table with George held his tongue and waited.

George seemed calmed now. The anger and frustration left him for a moment. He felt some of the men shifting to his side and them that didn't, he found he didn't care about. He'd show them he was right.

"I'm telling yer," he said, quieter. "There's somert gone on. Somert bad, and I'm gonna find out what."

*

Joseph walked back up the lane, Bess's paws quick on the ice and slush by the edges of the long grass. The darkness had covered the air now and as he reached the dip and curve of the road, Joseph held his face up towards the stars in the black sky. He felt them move and crackle in his vision and he closed his eyes against them for no more than a second. For that brief moment nothing else mattered. He was just a man. A man walking in his home lands, the vast sky above him, the mysterious stars pulsing.

Then Bess barked and Joseph opened his eyes and looked down at her. She'd seen something. Something in the lane ahead. Maybe a fox, he thought. He whispered, "What is it, Bess?" Then he saw the movement himself. It was a man. Or at least it was a person. The bushes shifted and the figure seemed to flit. It was too dark to see properly, but the movement was that of a shadow, a drifting darkness within the darkness of the night.

Joseph peered into the bushes but he could no longer tell if the person was there or not. It felt like the harder he stared, the less he could make out.

He recalled the same movement of a person, shadowy, down through the trees while he saw to Sarah and the earth, the shortest break in his work with the spade. And he had the terrible feeling of something coming, of trouble building and being onto him. Of being found out.

He moved fast, like he always did, without too much thought to his actions. He set off running towards the bushes where the figure had moved, Bess running ahead of him and barking into the night. His feet skidded on the ice and slush, and Bess disappeared into the bush, her brown tail slithering between branches and leaves. Joseph was at the bushes, his hands clawing at them to see through and get at whoever was there.

"Bess!" he called. He couldn't hear her at all. He knew if she'd found someone there she'd be barking all her suspicion out into the night air. But she was quiet, and it worried Joseph even more. He stopped his movement and listened. "Bess!" he called again. There was a rustling and Joseph was frozen like the ground he stood on. He peered into the bush and waited to see a form emerge. A man perhaps. Someone who had it in for him. Someone who knew. He tried to follow the sound of the rustling as it came closer. Then he found his attention was pulled down, and Bess appeared from the branches and leaves. She was wagging her tail and as Joseph leaned down to pet her he noticed she carried something in her mouth. He glanced again at the bushes but couldn't detect any movement or any person there now. He held the scruff of Bess's neck and led her away from the bush. "There now, girl," he said quietly. He led her into the lane and looked down on her in the moonlight. The moon was shaded in the sky above him and Joseph touched Bess's face where she held something in her teeth. Joseph frowned as he looked at his dog. She held a wide thick damp piece of wood. No longer than an arm bone, but as dense as a leg's, and stripped of all its outer skin. Joseph tried to take the log from her but Bess growled low when he did. Her ears went back and a snarl lingered around her mouth. He let her keep it. He was puzzled by it, but it was only a piece of wood. No harm.

Joseph carried on in the lane and back to the house, glancing at Bess every now and then. She carried the piece of wood all the way home, into the house, and dropped it where she slept. It was only then, when she let it go, that Joseph was able to get a better look at it. It was just a piece of wood, but one side of it had been shaved clean with a blade, and on this pale area Joseph was able to make out lines scored into the wood with the same blade. It meant nothing to Joseph, just lines crossed over here and there, a scattering of thoughts gouged into the soft wood. It meant nothing but, still, Joseph didn't take the piece of wood away from Bess. Whatever it was, she seemed more attached to it now than the moon to the night sky.

*

George left the Kingston Arms with his blood heavy with beer. He knew what he knew. He knew he was right. It was a bad business and it was up to him to get to the bottom of it and set things straight. As much as he could.

He'd been one of the last to leave the Low Drop. Most

of the men became uncomfortable with the talk and mumbled about how bad the weather was and how they'd get back to their wives and their firesides and their beds. George had no wife anymore. George's wife had died years ago along with the only child he'd ever fathered. Now his bed was never warm and his fire was un-kept.

George had looked on Sarah for the last couple of years as the only woman who might take his wife's place. He dreamed of it. He'd seen her in his mind through the days with him, by his side and in his bed.

Now no one knew where she was, but George knew what he knew. He knew where she'd been and most likely what had happened to her. He just needed to hear it. He needed a witness.

The walk up the lane was an easier one tonight. The snow was moving on and the air wasn't thick with it like it had been the previous nights. And yet, the walk up the lane seemed to ask so much of him tonight. He walked as if he was walking to his own death; the promise of the information he sought was heavy on him, though he needed it.

He reached the place where the road dipped and curved. He made his way down from the lane, ahead of the cluster of bushes and trees, and walked until he found the stream. This was the way he knew to the hovel the old woman and her son lived in. Set away from the village and beneath the hill shaped like a tipped-up anvil. By the flow of the stream, and hidden to the left. George had first been here when his wife died. Grief was like a dark veil on his days and he thought he would die himself if he didn't get some help. The old woman had surprised him by talking about the moon and the stars above and how George would go through a journey of emotions just like the journey of the moon and sun each day. She gave him a bottle of liquid to take each evening which she said would ease his grief and help him sleep. And it did.

Before that, his wife had been to the old woman when she first suspected the child was growing in her. The old woman had confirmed it and had given her some instructions on staying well. She'd told his wife to fetch her when the pains were strong and she would bring the baby into the world, like she had done for many other women. But, when the time came, the birth had come on so fast there was nothing George could do to get help. His neighbours had done what they could and two women from the village had attended her, but she died anyway, and the baby. There'd been no time for him to get to the old woman, and those who attended his wife that day had seemed so preoccupied with what they were doing, by the time the old woman was brought it was too late. Still, when she did come, she sat by his wife for hours and repeated words under her breath. She wrapped the baby in cloth from the village, leaving the child in its mother's arms, and took the remains of the birth away with her.

But the old woman was close to death herself now and her son seemed to have taken over the role. So far, George found he could put as much of his trust and faith in the son as he did the mother.

George walked by the stream and felt the cold air on his numbed face. He reached the hovel and knocked.

*

Aaron went to the door and peered through a crack to see who was there. He was as sure as he could be that Joseph Bradshaw wouldn't have found his way down here. Aaron had quietened the man's dog when it came sniffing its way through the bushes, calmed it and spoken softly to it, looked into the animal's brown eyes, whispered in its ear and lain a chant on a nearby log before gifting it into the dog's eager jaw.

He was sure as he could be that they had carried on home.

Aaron hesitated when he saw George standing outside in the dark night. The last time he'd seen this man, the anger that bled from him was enough to make him never want to encounter him again. But Aaron knew he would have to. He knew him and his mother wouldn't last the winter out if he didn't do what had to be done.

He opened the door and greeted George. He could see immediately that the man had taken his fair share of drink tonight. Aaron weighed quickly in his mind all the possibilities. The man's anger and his drunkenness were stones caught in a wheel. But there was a way, if Aaron was careful, that he could take these things and hold them in his palm and shake them the way he wanted.

He invited George in and asked him to keep quiet on account of his mother being asleep and very old now.

"Right," George said. "Yes, yer mother were good to mi wife when she..."

Aaron knew about George's wife and smoothed the edges of his remembered grief. "Yes," he said. "My mother spoke fondly of your wife."

"Aye," George nodded. "Yer mother is a good woman." He paused and seemed to think, then motioned to Aaron. "And you," he said. "I reckon yer a good man. You 'elped me before."

Aaron took his words cautiously. "I'm happy if I could help."

"Aye," George continued. "Yer did. And now I need yer 'elp again."

"Sir, I can't help you with the lady in question."

"No!" George put in. "Yer can't. I know. And you know. You know why yer can't!"

Aaron frowned.

"We both know she can't be 'elped now, don't we?"

Aaron put his fingers to his face and felt at his beard. He thought about his mother's words – see all and say nowt – then he thought about their situation in this cold winter, and how he would cope when his mother was gone.

"What is it you want of me?" he asked.

"I want yer to tell me where she is."

Aaron could feel the stones of the man's anger and drunkenness slowing in his grasp. "Hmm. Maybe I can help you with this," he said. "But I fear now is not a good time."

"What d'yer mean?" George shouted. "Now's as good a time as any."

Aaron shushed him. "To see the whereabouts of Sarah Vernon is not so easy," he said. "It takes... time."

George stared at him. "Time?" he said. "But yer do know what's 'appened to 'er, don't yer?"

Aaron held his nerve and didn't answer. George seemed to receive the light of the situation in one moment of clearness.

"It's money yer want," George said suddenly. "Aye, I see. It's money. Yer mother never asked for money, but if that's 'ow it is..." And he went in his pockets and pulled coins out. Some fell to the floor and he bent to pick them up. As he stood straight again he saw Aaron peering down at him from below his eyelashes. "My mother accepted gifts as payment," he said. "But I fear we can no longer go on like that." His fingers about his chin, a confident look on his face. He took the coins from George and seemed to think a further minute. Then he said, "I do know what's happened to the young woman you ask about. I've seen it." And he touched the side of his own head now. "If you suspect someone of doing her harm, which I think you do, then you are right."

George stared at him in the barely lit room. "I am?" he asked.

"Yes," Aaron replied. "And you already have the name of the man who has done this to her."

Today

Glenn was such a dog. He got her every time. Not that she minded. Not that she cared. She was here with him, wasn't she? She wanted it as much as he did, didn't she?

While he showered, Lorraine packed her things in the overnight bag she'd brought with her. She took the necklace with the ruby drop in her hand and ran its delicate chain through her fingers. It was cool to the touch, sending a thrill through her warm skin. When she placed a necklace like this around her neck the heavy drop of the stone gave her a feeling of pleasure that bordered on sexual. She wondered if she was just as bad as Glenn when it came down to it. She turned the necklace in her hand. The settings of the stone were carved and shaped like a close-up snowflake. She wondered if it was hand-made. She'd ask Glenn when he came out of the shower. Though he probably didn't know. Probably hadn't taken that much notice.

When it came down to it, she thought, she was as bad as Glenn. Of course she was. It was just that she was here for different reasons to him. Men and women always do things for different reasons. Men didn't always know that, but women did.

She was still sitting there looking at the necklace when he walked out of the bathroom. She glanced up at him. He thought he was irresistible. He really did. He held the towel around his head and shoulders, just revealing his drenched chest hair. She ran her eyes over his body and saw him stand up a little straighter. He really did think he was God's gift.

He nodded to her hand. "You like it, then?" he asked.

"Of course," she said. "Is it hand-made?"

"Huh?"

She looked at his face. His browned skin. His dark hair with grey raked through it now. His narrow eyes.

"Is it hand-made?" she asked again.

"I don't know," he said. "Does it matter?"

She swayed her head as if she was thinking about it. "No," she said. "Just wondered if it was a one-off, you know, don't want to be bumping into anyone wearing the same jewellery as me. I'm unique, you know that."

Glenn gave a little smile and rubbed his hair with the towel again. "Oh, don't you worry," he said. "You won't know anyone who could afford one of those."

He walked around the bed and began to dress. Lorraine still sat there, playing with the necklace in her hand.

"Where does Julia think you are right now, then?" she asked.

"We don't talk about Julia," he answered.

"I was just asking."

She was quiet again, still fingering the necklace in her hand.

"What would she say if she knew?"

Glenn stopped dead, his shirt in his hands, where he stood, and stared at her. Lorraine let the silence rest for a second, then she turned where she sat and looked up at him.

"I mean, couldn't she find out you were buying someone presents?"

"No," he said. "I'm careful, and anyway she doesn't check my personal money."

"Personal money?"

"Yeah, you know, we have a joint account and all that, but I have my own money as well, she doesn't know about that."

"She doesn't know?"

Lorraine was still looking up at him from the bed, but she could feel that she was close to the edge of the words he would allow.

"Why are you asking me all this?" he said. "You know I don't like to talk about Julia and you know she can never find out. She'd ruin me."

"But if you have your own money..."

"Not that kind of money," he snapped. Then he began to put his shirt on, and his words softened again. "I have my own money, yeah, for things like this, things she doesn't need to know about, expensive watches and nights away and things for you, little holidays, but..." He started buttoning his shirt up, watching Lorraine sitting on the bed. "You know, me and Julia, we've got the big house with the land and everything, and the business and... she'd take my bloody pension, she'd take everything she could."

He was getting agitated again. He lifted the collar of his shirt stiffly.

"And we wouldn't want that," Lorraine said.

"No, we bloody wouldn't."

Glenn walked back around the bed and into the bathroom. As he passed her, Lorraine glanced to the right and saw the free-standing mirror that had so spooked her the night before. She caught her own reflection as Glenn moved in front of her. Her long dark hair, her fake tan, her manicured nails and her waxed legs. It took a lot of upkeep. It cost a lot to look this good. And she liked the way she looked. She stared at herself and smiled. "No, we wouldn't," she whispered.

*

The receptionist hardly looked at Lorraine when they checked out. But she was used to that. Probably jealous anyway, she thought again. Bet she never got a ruby necklace bought for her as a simple present from a man, no reason other than he could, not because he had to, but because he wanted to. Bet she never got anything like that.

Glenn was giving the big key back. It clunked on the desk as he put it down.

"Don't very often get actual keys these days," he said. "But I'm sure you get a lot of people saying that."

Lorraine looked at him. Was he flirting?

The receptionist smiled. "We're an old inn, sir, even the doors to the rooms are old, so we have to have keys. And no, to be honest, not many people take the time to say much."

Lorraine looked at the woman. Was she blushing? She looked from one of them to the other. They wouldn't notice if Lorraine turned into a bloody sheep. They were flirting. Lorraine wasn't having this. It was her night away. Her night with Glenn. She was the one he bought presents for and paid attention to, and if he was going to flirt with anyone it would be her, not some cheap receptionist. And, come to think of it, if this cheap receptionist wanted to have a cute little conversation it would be with Lorraine and not Glenn. Lorraine did not like being ignored and left out. She leaned on the desk a little and the woman glanced at her. Lorraine looked down at the woman's name badge. "So... *Monica*, just how old is this place?" Lorraine asked.

If she wasn't blushing before she was now. "Erm... well, it dates back to the nineteenth century, I think."

Lorraine put her elbow on the desk and leaned her chin on it as if she was bored. "Oh right, like in those pictures over there?" She stretched out her arm behind her towards the wall with the pictures on. The woman hesitated. "Yes," she answered.

Glenn had noticed what she was doing. He'd moved away from the desk and grasped the handle of his overnight bag tightly. He was getting impatient now. But Lorraine wasn't done yet. The way he was so obviously embarrassed amused her.

"So," she went on. "What's that other picture? The dark one."

The woman looked over at the wall. "Well, I'm not sure. Some of those are of the village."

"The ones that are paintings, or sketches or whatever?"

"I suppose."

"You don't know much about it, do you, Monica, to say you work here? But maybe you haven't worked here long, maybe you're not used to it all yet, maybe you've never seen a good-looking, well-hung, married, rich man before... or his well-kept screw on the side."

The woman was blushing again. Glenn had picked up his overnight bag and was moving towards the door. He was huffing with the slightest edge of annoyance and turning his back on Lorraine's little game when another, older woman walked through from the bar. She was about fifty, Lorraine guessed, with set, honey-blonde hair and rings on her browned, bony hands. Lorraine wondered if Julia looked anything like this.

Monica was almost on her feet now, her chair being pushed back behind her as she tried to shift the conversation away from herself. She was clearly flustered by Lorraine, and Lorraine smiled. The girl had gone bright red. Probably never met anyone quite like Lorraine before. Probably never had anyone speak to her like that before.

"Oh," she said to the woman." This... *lady* was just asking about the sketches of the village, weren't you?"

Lorraine looked at her, then turned to the older woman.

"Yes," she said. "That's right, I was."

"Lovely," the older woman said. "Any in particular?"

Glenn had walked out of the door now, shaking his head and muttering to himself. He was probably sitting in the car waiting already. She'd be damned if she scuttled out now and gave him the satisfaction of seeing even the tiniest amount of embarrassment on her face.

"That one there," Lorraine said, pointing again. "That right dark one."

The older woman looked up and followed her finger towards the wall. "Oh that," she said. "Yes, that's the village, before this old hotel was even built."

"Right," Lorraine went on. "So, what's going on in that picture? It looks weird."

"Oh, it's weird alright," the older woman said. "It's a picture of something that happened right here in the village, over two hundred years ago."

"What?" Lorraine asked. "What happened?"

The older woman smiled. "Oh, there's a story," she said.

Derbyshire, 1760s

It was past midnight when George stood banging on Mr
Vernon's door. Mrs Vernon was a meek creature, some said
ill, some said mad, who hardly ever ventured out of the house
and was seldom seen. George knew she wouldn't show her
face to his knocking. He knew it would be Mr Vernon he'd
get.

When he appeared at the door Mr Vernon didn't look
like a man who'd been disturbed of his sleep. He was fully
clothed and he stared out of the house and rubbed his chin, the
two day growth prickly under his fingers.

"What's tha want at this 'our?" he asked.

"I've got news," George answered. "About Sarah."

What George told Mr Vernon that night, sitting by his
fire and relaying all he knew so far, was a tale no father would
want to hear about his daughter.

"Not my Sarah," The father said at first. And he gazed
into the fire and shook his head. "My Sarah wouldn't go about
like that. She's a good girl. She wouldn't, not with another
woman's 'usband. Not at all. Not with anyone. Not Sarah."

George leaned forward and laid his hands on the other
man's by the fire. "Nay!" he said. "It weren't Sarah's fault.
It's all 'im. Bradshaw. 'E's to blame for this. All of it. 'E's 'ad
'is way and then..."

Mr Vernon looked up quickly, his pleading eyes
desperate for this to be some mistake. He seemed to hesitate as
all George had said worked inside of him. Then he looked to
the fire again. "If 'e's done for 'er, like yer say 'e 'as, I'll see
'im 'ang."

George breathed deeply now, sure he had this one
person at least on his side. And he needed no other. Not really.
The two of them could see to this.

"Come with me, tomorrow, and we'll get the lad to tell
us what Bradshaw's done with 'er. 'Is mother is old and near
death, and 'e wants money, but 'e sees things, I'm telling yer.
'E knows what's 'appened 'ere."

Mr Vernon nodded. "Alright," he said. "I'll come with

58

yer tomorrow and if this lad is right, and all 'e says is true, 'e can 'ave all the money I can fair give 'im."

*

The old woman wasn't opening her eyes much at all these last couple of days. Her breathing was shorter and pulled through her with a scratchy sound. Aaron stayed close to her while he was inside, listening to the sound of air in her lungs, feeling how much warmth was still in her skin, watching for a flicker of her eyelids or a murmur from her mouth.

He found that his own sleep bobbed like it was in water, under then rising again. But each time he woke and opened an eye to check on his mother she was still the same. By day he walked along by the stream, up the hills, through the fields and sometimes in the lane, while back inside his mother slept on. Aaron was beginning to think she would slip away like this, when he pulled himself up in the morning and shuffled over to sit by her and check her again. She didn't open her eyes, but said, "Why do you go wandering so much, lad?"

He stared at her a moment, half wondering if he'd just heard it in a dream. Then she sighed at the silence, impatient with his hesitation, as if she knew she didn't have time for this.

"I... I look around," he answered. "I collect the things you've told me about and I watch and I see things happening."

"What do you see?" she asked.

"I see some bad things, mother," he answered. "People aren't good. They don't look after each other."

"Aye, you're right there, lad. That's how people are. But that's not our business. See all and say nowt."

He looked at her then in the dim morning light. She was old, and things were changing, things she didn't understand. She would be gone soon and it would be up to him to decide for himself. Aaron already knew that he couldn't follow his mother in everything she said and believed. He knew it wouldn't be possible. He'd never survive. Besides, if people were bad, then what carried on couldn't be helped.

He thought she'd done talking and sleep had pulled her back under. He watched her for a moment longer then moved to get to his feet. Her hand came out and held his arm. She struggled to open her eyes and look at his face.

"Aaron," she said. "I'll be gone soon. It's up to you now, lad. You have to carry on. Folk round here will expect it. They'll look to you to take my place and do all that I did for them. I'm passing it all to you now, lad."

She took his hand in hers and patted it, then held it tightly. Aaron had the strangest feeling. He closed his eyes and let all her energy flow into him. All her wisdom. All her knowledge. Her gift.

Aaron's mother didn't die that day, but she didn't speak to him again. Aaron knew talking was an effort for her now and he didn't press her. She would die the next day, and in the time that passed in between Aaron couldn't be sure if she could even hear him. He still spoke to her though. Aaron had a lot on his mind. A lot to bother him and keep him awake even when his mother was dead and he no longer woke to check her. He had other things making his sleep bob to the surface on and off all night.

The next day that passed, before his mother died, Aaron talked to her more than he had in years, and, although she didn't speak back, Aaron felt he knew her mind. He knew what she would say if she could. And he knew she was wrong.

*

They walked up past the Low Drop, snow compacting and crunching under their feet. They saw the sign, "The Kingston Arms", sway slightly in the winter breeze, heard it creak, breathed in the complicated smell of hops. Past the gate to the church, where Mr Vernon had encountered Anne Bradshaw, ice in his feet and heavy worry in his body. He thought of her now, of how she had seemed that day, the look on her face when she saw him. Guilt. He was sure of it. Even the pastor had been unsettled. As if he knew. Maybe everybody knew, he thought. Maybe he was an old fool and everybody knew.

They walked up the lane, away from the clutch of houses, the ground slippery and frozen under their feet. The air cold and the sky white. Up the dip and bend in the road. Here they cut from the road and walked down by the bushes, the grass wet and difficult with snow, icy where it had been trodden before, thick and cumbersome where it had not.

The two men came upon the stream, flowing through the cracks in the ice, determined, unstoppable. They walked until they came to the hovel, sheltered by the hill and hidden by the landscape.

They stopped and looked at each other. Neither man spoke but they could each feel the words. If either of them were unsure, wanted to back out and forget all about this, now was the time. But neither of them could see a future that way. Neither of them would ever sleep again if they didn't follow through with this.

They nodded to each other and George stepped forward and knocked on the door.

*

Aaron stood and peered out. He could see the two men waiting, their heads bowed in the cold air, their faces tight with nerves. The skin of their cheeks and noses was blooming red against the freezing wind and they moved their bodies, one foot to the other, to prevent their toes from losing sensation.

He opened the door and asked them to come inside. The three men stood together inside, the old woman's breathing the only sound for a moment.

"How is your wife?" Aaron asked.

Mr Vernon glanced at George and hesitated. "Er... she is well... as can be expected."

Aaron nodded, his face serious. "Yes," he said. "'Tis difficult times."

George leaned forward and interrupted. "Aye, well, that's why we're 'ere. We want to know what 'e's done with her, Sarah, we want to know where she is."

Aaron let the silence settle. He felt the power of information swell inside him. Most probably no one except himself and Joseph Bradshaw knew the answer to this question. This was valuable.

He addressed Mr Vernon. "You want peace of mind?" he asked.

Mr Vernon nodded firmly. "Aye."

"I can help you with that," Aaron said.

Then he waited. He stood in silence, his fingers in the hair of his beard, looking at the two men. Waiting.

George was the first to react. "We've got money." And he brought out some coins and pushed them into Aaron's hand.

Aaron weighed the coins in his palm. He glanced around at his mother just once then he said to the men, "Very well. But let's go outside, my mother is sleeping and I don't want to wake her."

*

Aaron walked ahead of the two men, following the stream further than they had gone before. He walked where the water ran slowly by the hills, the two men behind him, their feet unsteady with the sound of the stream constantly by them. Then, without a word, Aaron turned to the left and walked towards the lane, up, up where the sky stretched out and met the dark horizon. There he stopped and turned to face them. The two men stood before him, waiting as if standing before their own fathers as boys. Aaron breathed in and felt the power again. Larger than before, even. More potent. He felt the great sky behind him where he was standing, the frozen ground under his feet, the land all around him.

He looked from one man to the other and without looking behind him, he said, "You see the place where the trees shade the sky?"

The two men just stared at him for a second, bewildered expressions flitting on their faces. Aaron turned his head to the left a little and the men's gazes followed.

He took a deep breath. It was more difficult than he had imaged. The girl's father was waiting for him to speak, and he would have to be the one to tell him. But it wriggled inside him and wouldn't come out straight.

"Where the trees meet the sky," he said. "Bradshaw's cattle roam closely."

The two men waited, hanging on his words.

"Yes?" George said.

Aaron sighed and looked directly at Mr Vernon. "Sir, your daughter lies there," he said. "Bradshaw took a spade and dug down between the trees and buried her there. I have seen it."

Today

Glenn was already in the car before the woman had finished telling her story to Lorraine. She was frowning by the time she came out of the hotel, opened the car door and slid in beside him.

"What was all that about?" he asked.

"Huh?"

"You in there just now, it was embarrassing."

"Oh, I'm sorry!" she said. "It was embarrassing for you, was it? Well how do you think I felt watching you flirt with the bloody receptionist?"

"I wasn't flirting."

"Come on."

"Well, whatever, it's no reason to show yourself up like that."

"I wasn't showing myself up. For your information, I was having a conversation."

"Oh yeah, that's right, you were having a normal conversation, chatting with them about them pictures and shit. Don't make me laugh, Lorraine, you hate other women."

Lorraine turned sharply to look at him. "What do you mean, I hate other women? I do not."

"Yeah you do. Like you'd be just having a conversation like that. Come on, how many women friends do you have?"

She scowled. "That doesn't mean I hate women!"

Glenn shrugged. "Alright, alright," he said. "So what was it all about, then?"

"What was what about?"

"Your conversation."

"She was telling me about the picture, the sketch or whatever."

Glenn started the engine and turned the car out of the car park. "What about it?"

The car moved slowly around and the stone building and the hotel passed by Lorraine's window. "It was about the village," she said. "Something that's supposed to have

64

happened there ages ago, I mean like a-a-ages ago."

"What's that then?"

Lorraine followed the building as the car moved away from it. "Young woman was having it off with this married man and he murdered her."

Glenn glanced at her. "Why?" he asked.

"They don't know, but I mean, you can guess, can't you? He was having his cake and eating it, wasn't he? She probably wanted more than he would give her."

"All women do," Glenn muttered. "So, that's what the picture was about? A murder?"

"Oh no, the picture was about what happened after that."

*

They are talking and he takes a left at the little mini-roundabout. Down. Down the road ahead, sudden like the curl of a rollercoaster, and into a village. They come upon a small row of shops, just four or five, and a pub. Behind, more to the left, they can see the tall stretch of a church.

"Shit. I've taken a wrong turn."

"Are you sure?" She looks at him and sees his eyes darting from left to right and his teeth taking the corner of his mouth and holding it there.

"Yeah, we didn't come through here, did we? Think I should have gone straight on back there. Keep your eyes peeled."

"For what?"

"Road signs. Anything. Just keep looking."

"Can't you turn round?"

"Yeah, when I can find somewhere, these old roads are so bloody narrow."

He's pretty calm so far, but Lorraine can feel his annoyance over the wrong turn. She can feel it like winter in the air outside, like suspicion in a look, like a glance in a crowd. She turns her face away from him in the car. To say they'd been to the best hotel he'd ever taken her to, it hadn't exactly been a success. She'd been sulky and irritated and jealous, and... scared. All totally ridiculous, and the latter two things, at least, she never normally was. It was that place, she was sure of it. They were better off in the dumpy hotel in town, with its lumpy pillows and threadbare sheets and the TV that never worked. That hotel they'd been to last night had done something to her, altered her mood, made her jumpy. It had a bad atmosphere.

She shakes her head at herself. Can't believe she is thinking like this. It's ridiculous. That hotel last night was way better than the one in town. It was the sort of place Glenn should be taking her. With his money. Can't believe she is actually thinking she prefers the dump in town just because he flirted with the receptionist and Lorraine got freaked out by some noise in the night and...

She is looking from the car window. Doing what he said. Keeping her eyes peeled. They have passed the church and a few houses and are going up the hill at the other side of the village, away from it again, when she sees it.

Not "it". Her.

When she sees her. The same girl she'd seen in the mirror in the middle of the night in the hotel, when the headlights from passing cars swooped through the hotel room, when no one could have been there, when she couldn't have seen anything at all.

Lorraine turns her body round fully in her seat, seat belt straining across her middle. "Did you see her?" she says.

Glenn looks from the road to Lorraine and back again. "What? Who?"

"That girl. Did you see her?"

"No. What girl?"

Lorraine is still looking behind her, but bushes have covered the spot and the road curves around. "That girl just then, standing by the side of the road."

"No. I didn't see anybody. We're supposed to be finding our way back to the right road, not looking out for lost kids."

Lorraine begins to straighten her body in the seat, but still looks over her shoulder. "She wasn't a kid," she murmurs. Then she turns to Glenn. "What was that village?"

66

He eyes her quickly. "Huh? I don't know, just a wrong turn."

She can feel his impatience with her, but it doesn't matter, she isn't bothered. "What was it called?"

"I don't know," he answers. "Does it matter?"

But she doesn't reply. She is thinking about the girl, the one standing by the road just now, the one in the mirror last night. Stupid. It couldn't be the same girl. Obviously. And yet... and yet she's sure it is. As sure as she is about anything. Lorraine thinks how strange it is that she isn't scared now. How different it feels this morning. How everything is always more bearable in daylight. She would go as far as to say she feels quite calm. And things were slotting into place, slowly, in her head. It was the same girl. The one she'd seen reflected in the mirror last night. The one the woman at the hotel told her about, giving her body to a man who gave her nothing in return, who used her and then disposed of her. Lorraine looks at Glenn quickly as he turns off the road at the top of the next hill and back into the right direction to take her home. Lorraine would never let that happen to her.

Derbyshire, 1760s

The weather was breaking. Anne had been up soon after Joseph. First sitting in the bed and gazing out of the bedroom window, over the fields shaped like a full belly and still and white as a queen. Then about the house, cleaning up after Bess and preparing lunch for Joseph. She could see from the window at the back of the house that the snow wasn't falling anymore and what was left on the ground was becoming softer and easier to cope with. Joseph had gone from the house without a word, the only evidence of him being the sound of the door as he closed it behind him and the scratch of Bess's paws on the floor as she followed him around. At around eight Anne put on her coat, straightened her hair down with her hand and fixed her mind, and left the house.

She didn't walk to the dip and bend in the road or past the Low Drop or the church. She walked in the other direction. Away from the village. She hoped she wouldn't see anyone today, so early and heading towards the barren tops, but no sooner had she left the end of the path than the wife of the landlord from the Kingston Arms was in the lane. The woman was harsh and the last person Anne would want to see. They stared at each other for the briefest moment before the woman shouted, "You'd show yer face out of t'ouse? After what yer 'usband's been up to!"

Anne could feel the hotness filling her neck and face. Her breath came out fast against the cold air.

"Aye, I've 'eard," the woman went on. "We've all 'eard. 'Im and Sarah Vernon. And where is she now, eh?" The woman pointed to Anne, her arm outstretched towards her. "I'll bet my arm you know!"

Anne turned away from the woman, sickness rising in her throat and a heavy pull in her limbs. She moved to walk away, the woman's words following her in the cold morning air.

"'Ear this, Anne Bradshaw!" she shouted. "It'll all be known. Yer 'usband'll get what's coming to 'im."

As she walked away, Anne's hands shook like the legs

of a dying cow. She told herself it was the cold, but the shock of the woman's violent words ran in her mind and through her body. For the moment, all she wanted was to be as far away from those people as possible.

She carried on up, until Joseph's fields were behind her and the village wasn't visible anymore. Here it was like another world. The land here was craggy with stone. A great scattering, like the angels above had played skittles with rocks. The peaks held the snow firmly to them, the wind circled and the sky hung low. Here everything felt different. Anne always thought so. Up here, away from all else, she could see clearly and breathe easily. The humps and drops in the landscape could be dangerous if you didn't know. But Anne knew. She'd walked it often enough.

On the other side, almost at the next village, she could feel the change inside her. A tension and stress replacing the shock of the landlord's wife before, and rising in her middle. If only she could stay with the rocks and the high peaks, the sky long and close to her.

Anne thought about what she would say to her mother for a while before she reached the house. Practised the words and phrases in her head until they sounded silly and foreign. By the time she got to the door her words were a scramble inside her.

"Anne," her mother said. "Come in, Anne, come in."

She stepped into the house she was born in and felt a strange displacement. She was changed somehow by all that had happened lately, and the old comfort of this house and her mother seemed gone.

Her mother made tea and Anne helped her with her laundry. The two women were quiet for a time and then Anne said, "Mother, were you ever afraid of father?"

Her mother looked up from the clothes, startled by the question. "Of course not! What a question!"

They were quiet again and Anne kept her eyes on the clothes. But the thoughts ran in her and she looked up again. "Did 'e ever do things...?"

Her mother put the clothes down firmly and stared at

her daughter. "Anne, really! What is wrong with yer?"

Anne couldn't look at her mother at first. She kept her face turned towards the clothes. There were too many things moving in her head. Too many questions and worries and uncertainties.

"Joseph, 'e..." Then she stopped. She couldn't tell her mother all that had happened. It was hard enough to think about it, but trying to speak it made a thunder of emotion begin inside her. She considered her mother, and her own shame. She wrapped all the terrible things that had happened recently tightly together and she laid them down somewhere deep in her head and her heart. She took a breath. "I 'ope to be 'aving a bairn," she said at last. She looked up at her mother and the woman still had a confused expression about her eyes, but it melted away when she saw her daughter's face.

"Well then," she said. "It's quite normal to feel... unsure and... frightened perhaps, but all will be well, Anne, children are a great blessing and you will make a fine mother."

Anne smiled and looked to the laundry again. Her mother seemed lifted by the idea of a baby coming, even though it was only an idea, and she began to chat with a leap in her words.

"I remember when I were carrying you, 'ow attentive your father was, treated me like I were a babe meself!" She laughed at the memory as she spoke it. "And me sister were 'aving one at t'same time, and she said, 'ow he loves you, that 'usband of yours, and she said that 'ers weren't nowt like that, and..." Then her mother stopped suddenly. "Eee," she said. "I know I 'ave somert to tell you. You remember yer cousin, Thomas, don't yer? Me sister's lad."

Anne said she did.

"'E's the one she were 'aving when I were 'aving you. Well, there's been a to-do over 'im, I can tell yer. Me poor sister is almost dead with worry over it."

"Why? What's 'appened?"

"'E's only been caught, drunk as yer like and fair mad with his shotgun. Almost killed Mr Morton down 'ere."

"What? Why?"

Anne's mother waved her hand as if wafting the suggestion away. "Ow, he didn't mean it, 'e were just drunk. Yer remember him, don't yer? 'E were always like that. Always 'andful. Anyway, 'e came round 'ere the next evening and fair pleaded with yer father to 'elp 'im."

Anne's eyes were wide as she stared at her mother and listened to her speak.

"Said 'e never meant for the thing to go off and certainly din't mean to shoot anyone. Though 'e 'ad to admit to being drunk. Anyway, 'e asked for yer father's 'elp. Sat right in this 'ouse 'ere and asked 'im straight out!"

"Why father?"

"On account of 'is reading, of course. Thomas might not be the brightest, but 'e knows 'e can get off if 'e can prove 'e can read. All 'e's got to do is learn the psalm and 'e can claim that benefit of clergy. 'E knows yer father can teach 'im." She motioned to Anne. "You know that, 'e taught you to read, din't 'e?"

Anne nodded. "Yes," she said quietly. "'E did."

*

Aaron moved away from the two men. He'd observed a changing of emotions on Mr Vernon's face and he worried about being blamed for bringing him the news. But Mr Vernon seemed to forget that Aaron was even there. Tears and immediate grief and shock all came to the man's face, then anger as well. He tore at his own head as if he could tear the information out.

"I'll kill 'im!" he shouted. Then he took hold of George's clothes and hung onto him, the two men's faces close together. "We'll go up there now and 'av'im!"

George was the one who calmed the man. Aaron watched from a few paces away now, as George spoke as if speaking to a child, laying his hands on Mr Vernon's arms and shushing him. "No, wait. Think on it," he said. "We'll 'av'im alright, we'll see 'im done for, but we 'av to use our 'eads."

Mr Vernon stared into George's eyes as if George held all the knowledge he needed and he might find it this way.

"We munt go to Bradshaw," George said. "We go straight t't'magistrate. To Inkerswell. We do this proper, and that way we see Bradshaw 'ang for what 'e's done."

*

Aaron felt a heaviness pulling at him as he walked away from the two men. He'd been paid for his information and the two men believed him, but he still felt an indescribable sadness at the whole sorry business. He reasoned he'd done the right thing. Mr Vernon deserved to know what had happened to his daughter. Joseph Bradshaw deserved to hang. But Aaron still felt uncomfortable. Maybe because he hadn't been completely honest with the two men.

As he walked back home he knew he would find his mother dead when he got there. He knew she wanted to be alone when she passed over and that she was waiting till the last moment, when she was sure Aaron wouldn't be back, to let herself go and slip over to the other side.

He approached the little hovel slowly, feeling as if his whole body was being dragged back. Back to the stream. Back to the hills. Back to the land and the wide open spaces he loved. He lowered his face in the cold air and made himself go forward into the hovel.

The atmosphere inside was changed. And he knew he'd been right and she was gone. He didn't need to check her breathing and make sure, but he did anyway. He closed the door behind him, feeling a drop in the air inside, and he walked slowly forward to his mother. He looked at her closely as he approached her. So strange. She looked the same yet, like she was sleeping. He knelt down next to her and carefully laid his hand on her chest. Nothing. He pressed further into her clothes and stayed as still as he could. Next he put his cheek to her face and waited to feel breath. None. She was dead. But he had known that before he got here. He took her hands in his. She was still warm and he looked at her and held the shortest moment of doubt. Then he let go.

*

Anne walked back home before lunch time. Sleet came down cold and wet on the top and she watched it fall as light hail onto the rocks beside the path for a few seconds. Then the wind seemed to take it away, blow it out over the grass, and she felt the sleet on her face again as she walked on.

The words her mother had spoken were a wheel in her head. She turned them over like her hands in dough. Anne felt as if she lived with a constant sickness in her stomach and a heavy stone in her belly these last couple of days, but thinking on her mother's words, she experienced a lifting and a rising of a smile inside her. It was the strangest feeling. Hers and Joseph's situation was surely a bad one, and yet she now felt a strange kind of happiness, or at least a lightness. There was yet the chance to make all this right. There was every chance Joseph would get off if Anne taught him the psalm. And she could do it. She could easily do it.

She came to the brow of the hill she walked on and slowed a little as she approached. Here she could see Joseph's fields, thick with snow still and cut by the low stone walls. He worked hard for this. He was a good man. She was sure of it. He wasn't perfect, but people on this earth rarely are. He was good at heart. She was sure.

She walked down towards the house, feeling the air soften and the sleet ease. All would be well. Anne would have a child and Joseph would be fine and all would be well. They'd forget about this bad business. This awful winter would be over and they would look forward once again.

Anne came to the path that led to her house when she noticed two women from the village in the lane. She stopped and looked over at them. For a moment Anne still held the lightness inside her, hope for the future and the leap of good faith, then she felt herself freeze where she stood as the two women stared right at her, their faces still and darkened, their eyes harsh, their mouths already tutting and whispering about her. They fixed Anne with the blackest looks, then, their eyes full of disgust, they turned away and walked out of the lane.

*

Joseph came into the house at lunch time. Bess padded forward, her paws slipping slightly on the floor, her breath hot and her tongue lazy in her mouth. Anne ran cold water into a bowl and set it down on the floor for the dog. She kept her back turned to Joseph as he sat to the table and waited. A silence buzzed between them, then Anne turned around and began cutting bread for his meal.

"I went to me mother's this morning," Anne said. She didn't look at Joseph's face, but kept her eye on the bread and the knife she used. He didn't answer. "She were telling me about me cousin Thomas, 'e's been arrested." She felt Joseph's eyes flit to her face quickly then, and she raised hers to meet him.

"What for?" he asked.

"Being drunk with a shotgun. 'E almost killed Mr Morton."

Joseph let go a small laugh and Anne felt the discomfort ruffle her. He thought this was funny.

"She told me 'e went to father for 'elp."

Joseph took the bread and began to eat roughly and hungrily. "Oh aye?" he said.

Anne nodded and sat down at the table opposite Joseph. She stretched out her arms across the table to meet his hands, but Joseph kept himself busy with the meal.

"She told me, as long as 'e learned the psalm 'e could claim the benefit of clergy."

Joseph stopped eating and stared at his wife over the table.

"You can do the same, Joseph. I can teach yer."

He chewed his food slowly now, still looking at her, then he lowered his eyes to the bread again. "I've not been arrested for owt," he mumbled.

"But yer will be," she answered. "Just this morning, out in the lane, I've 'ad stares and tuts and such dirty looks coming my way, Joseph, and t'wife of t'landlord from t'Low Drop shouted at me about you! They know somert's up, they won't leave it be, Joseph."

She could see an anger rising in him. His fingers

74

tightened to make half fists on the table and his mouth set firm.

"No one knows nowt!" he shouted. "They can say what they like." He hit one of his fists against the wooden table, stood up, pushed his chair away behind him, a quick whistle and Bess was alert to him, wagging her tail and watching him for a command. He walked from the house suddenly, Bess behind him, slamming the door as he left.

*

The cold seemed keener that afternoon. He knew he hadn't eaten as much as he'd have liked at lunch, but she would go on, she had to say something, didn't she? Couldn't help herself. He'd not been able to stay at the table then and talk with her and eat as if everything was fine. Some gossip in the village and she was letting her mind work over too much. What were a few looks? A few whispered words? An arrest didn't follow.

Joseph could hear his cattle moan, their feet sinking in skids of mud, the ground becoming boggy where the snow had begun to melt and the sleet had come down. He looked over to the trees behind the house. Joseph hadn't been up there since – the sight of it made him flinch and a strange jolt hit the insides of his chest. Sometimes when he went about his work he could almost feel the woods on the skin of his face, around his eyes and cheeks, as if they reached out and tore at his flesh.

He made himself look at it now. Made himself think about it. Really think about it. Because he thought about it all the time, but he constantly pushed it away, made it sit under the surface of his mind. Now he stood and looked at the woods and made himself think about the place where Sarah lay.

Someone had seen him that night. He couldn't be sure because it had been dark and all he'd seen of them was a movement, a figure, a shadow. But Bess had known someone was there. And all Bess knew was simple, honest truths.

What if Anne was right and people were talking? What if whoever had seen him that night had told? Joseph picked a stray rock up from the cold, wet ground and threw it at the nearest wall.

"Damn you, Sarah Vernon," he muttered to himself. "Damn you to hell."

*

It was dark when he went back to the house, as it always was after a day's work at this time of year. When he walked in, the darkness all round him and the stars behind him, Anne felt the same sense of low fear that she had the night he'd come in and told her about Sarah. She sat by the fire and looked at him. He stood in the doorway a moment, obedient Bess staying with him, till he stomped his boots to shake off the mud and slush from the fields and Bess padded forward to the fire.

Joseph closed the door behind him, took off his boots and coat and came slowly into the house.

"I've been thinking on what yer said," he told her.

Anne stared up at him, her eyes cautious in the glow from the fire. But Joseph was mild now and she soon knew she needn't fear him tonight.

"'Appen yer right," he went on. "'Appen we should... take care. I mean, if folk are talking, then..." He paused and Anne felt a smile rise inside her again. He needed her. "Wouldn't do no 'arm to learn the thing."

"I think so," she answered. "'Ere, come and sit down by t'fire and I'll fetch t'bible."

*

Anne opened the bible on her knee and found Psalm 51. They sat opposite each other, the fire playing with rubble in between them.

"Have mercy on me, O God, according to Your steadfast love," she began.

She saw Joseph close his eyes and breathe deeply through his nose. He pressed his fingers together in his lap and listened to Anne speak. He nodded his head. Anne could see, beneath his skin, the struggle with the words. He would have to ask for mercy. This wasn't something Joseph was used to doing. He would have to be humble and forget any idea of pride.

76

"Shall I read it whole to yer first?" she asked. "'Ow best do yer think yer'll remember it?"

He kept his eyes closed and something calm seemed to wash over him. An acceptance, maybe. Or maybe an understanding. The words she'd read sinking into his mind and laying a quieting in his blood. Anne thought he looked like he had some kind of peace now, maybe the most he'd had in days.

"Read on," he said.

She watched his face for a second and then turned back to the book she held on her knees. "According to Your abundant mercy, blot out my transgressions. Wash me thoroughly from my iniquity and cleanse me from my sin."

She looked up from the bible to check he was listening. He was gazing at her, the flames from the fire making patterns on his cheek.

"It will be alright, Joseph," she said. "I'll see that it will."

He smiled. He almost seemed meek now. "Yer a good woman," he said.

"Aye, that I am," she answered. "And don't you forget it, Joseph Bradshaw."

She could feel the subtle shift in the air then. A line between them that fizzed and altered. Positions shifting.

"Shall we carry on?" she said. "You need to learn this Joseph, if we are to save yer neck."

*

Later that night Joseph took Anne to bed in a way she couldn't remember him doing for years, if ever at all. He loved her gently and then lay behind her, his arms wrapped around her, his body curled against her. Anne lay in the darkness, feeling Joseph's sturdy arm, stroking his skin and watching the moon shiver in the black sky. If only it could always be like this. If only they could stay right here in this bed, love each other forever and never have to leave.

She stroked her hand down Joseph's arm and found her own stomach. She cupped her palm and fingers under the small swell of her belly. The child she longed for would grow here now. She was sure of it. Years later she would say that this was the night which made the baby. Because babies were made from love. They were pure. And this was the first night of pure love Anne thought she had ever had.

Today

Another pile of washing to do now she was back home. Another day of hoovering and making the bed and cleaning the bloody toilet. Another day of standing in front of the TV with the ironing board stretched out in front of her and the boredom itchy in her body. She wanted to go shopping. She wanted to be a lady who did lunch and spent long afternoons in expensive beauty salons. She looked at her petrol-blue polished nails, chipped and a little ragged round the edges, and put her fingers through her coarse, dry hair extensions. It all needed keeping up with. All needed maintaining. And her nails and hair were more important to her than how clean this stupid house was.

She stood in the bedroom and slowly pulled the zip on the overnight bag she'd taken to the hotel, and began taking out the clothes she'd worn and carefully folded when she'd packed them to come home.

The house Lorraine lived in with her husband was small. They'd rented this two-bedroomed rabbit hutch, as Lorraine sometimes called it, since they first moved in together, which was six months before they married, which was now three years ago. As much as Lorraine would like to move to something bigger, get a mortgage and own their own place, she knew it was unlikely. Lorraine couldn't see them ever being able to afford to move. If she brought it up and tried to push the point, Lorraine's husband would tell her he did his best. He'd say, carefully, that perhaps if she upped her hours at work, perhaps if she got a better job... but Lorraine didn't want to up her hours or get a better job. She didn't want a job at all.

She worked part-time in a small clothes store, though half the time she didn't bother turning up and everyone said she'd get the sack soon. She didn't care. Why should she care? She hated the stupid job anyway.

She unpacked everything in her overnight bag and took out the necklace Glenn had given her. She held it up in the light from the window like it had words and she was about to read them. It was nice. There was no denying it. Expensive too. Glenn had said as much. You won't come across anyone you know with one of these, he'd said. That meant, no one she knew could afford one. But Glenn could.

She passed the chain through her fingers and felt its cool, tingly metal awakening her skin.

Her husband wouldn't know. Wouldn't notice. He never did. As long as she made his tea for when he came in from work and always looked pretty, he didn't notice anything.

She laid the necklace in her jewellery box along with other things Glenn had bought her that her husband never noticed. Men were so stupid.

It was around the time Lorraine was sixteen that she had first known this. Lorraine's mother had struggled to bring Lorraine up on next to nothing after Lorraine's father had done a runner. He'd left them when times got tough, Lorraine's mother always said. Typical man, she said. When the shit hit, he was off. Didn't see him for dust. And her mother would wave her hand in a far-off way to show just how long gone he was.

Lorraine had accepted this story and laid it down inside herself. Didn't think about it much. Until she met men of her own. Then she saw the way things were. They wanted only one thing. Lorraine could give that, easily, but she wanted things in return. She wouldn't be like her mother. She was determined not to end up like her mother – no money, no life, no happiness.

Lorraine closed the jewellery box and looked around the bedroom. Of course, she married for security. She'd had to leave home as soon as she could. Better off out of it, anyway. And her mother couldn't afford to support her. She could have got a job, of course, but no job Lorraine could get would fund the lifestyle she wanted. So she'd married a man who would always be there for her. He was like the line of the horizon. Like the position of the sea. He was set in his ways, worked hard and would never leave her. Best of all, he didn't question her. Which just went to show how stupid men were.

She was just turning back to the chest of drawers her jewellery box sat on top of, just about to open the drawers and put away her comb and perfume and her make-up, when a soft bang in the doorway made her body jolt. She turned quickly to see the cat jumping from the bed onto the floor, catching the door before it leapt through and onto the landing. Just a second. That's all it was. Just a blink of an eye. And Lorraine had blinked her eyes. But just as the cat jumped and the door swayed, she could have sworn she saw someone standing there.

Derbyshire, 1760s

It came to him like the delicate wings of tiny midges on a spring breeze. Just a whisper at first. Just a thought. An idea. A rumour.

It reached his ears like the slow patter of summer rain on the ground below. Gossip in the village. His cook banging dishes as she wiped them and set her kitchen straight, her tongue loose with her disapproval.

"Mind, I'm not saying owt about her, 'cept she were always a one, that lass. I reckon it's on account of her mother being the way she is. No guidance, see?" She hung pans back on their hooks and pushed her hands down hard on her apron. "But 'im! Eey, if 'e were my 'usband 'e'd get what for."

He heard the words and he weighed them carefully in his serious mind. Gossip was always rattling around in the village, but there was something about this that made his breath feel hot in his lungs and his stomach tighten with disgust. Bradshaw. It was about that bull Bradshaw.

Mr Inkerswell had made little reaction so far to the rumours about Joseph Bradshaw and Sarah Vernon. Nothing about these tales surprised him, but he knew what people were like and Bradshaw was the kind of man who made enemies. He was surly. He was arrogant and bad tempered. He never gave an inch of his time to help others and always expected to gain peace. Still, mainly because of his position, Mr Inkerswell made no reaction to the gossip and kept his face evenly measured against it. Until this day.

On this day Mr Inkerswell was speaking to the parson. He had decided, as he often did, to visit his family's graves. He'd opened the gates and walked down the path towards the church. Mr Inkerwell's family, his mother, father and his late wife, were all buried close to one another behind the tall stone church, and he often visited them when he had the time. Sometimes he stood and spoke to his late wife. Sometimes in his head and sometimes, without always realising it, out loud. He'd just reached the side of the church and wasn't quite at the spot where his family were laid, when the parson came out of the church and walked towards him.

"A moment of your time," the parson had said.

Mr Inkerswell stopped for a second. It was inconvenient, but he never denied anyone who wished to speak with him, and nodded and walked indoors with the parson. The parson walked to the front of the church and motioned for Mr Inkerswell to join him in the pews.

"A delicate matter," the parson went on. "Perhaps you have heard the things being said about Joseph Bradshaw and Sarah Vernon."

Mr Inkerswell nodded again, but as yet kept quiet. He had found, in his time as magistrate here, that a little patience and an all-sweeping gaze could bring him more knowledge than the most in-depth conversation.

"The young woman's father is very upset..." the parson said. "As is her mother, of course, but the father, Mr Vernon... he is seeking answers as to the whereabouts of his daughter. You've heard the rumours, sir... he looks to Joseph Bradshaw, everyone here does, I think."

Mr Inkerswell kept his gaze on the eyes of the parson. The parson was probably the only one in the village right now, except for Anne Bradshaw, who didn't look with suspicion on Joseph, or he at least tried to keep his nose out of it.

"Yes," was all Mr Inkerswell said.

The parson stared back at him. "I just wanted to inform you of... the way the air is at this time. If Sarah isn't found..."

Mr Inkerswell nodded again. "I understand," he said. "You can rest assured, I will do all I can to get to the truth of the matter."

*

This was the day Mr Inkerswell felt himself pulled into the affairs of the Bradshaws and the Vernons. The gossip he had caught his cook whispering at the back door. The feeling on the cold winter breeze as he walked in the village. The way people carried themselves and the looks in their eyes. The absence of Joseph in the Kingston Arms, or more importantly the absence of both he and Anne in church.

And then Mr Vernon.

Then Mr Vernon came to him.

It was only a day after the parson had spoken with Inkerswell. Inkerswell was carefully running all the things the parson had said, and the gossip and the whispers he'd heard, backwards and forwards in his mind, shifting them and sifting through them like a hand in grain. Something had to be done, but with only rumour and worry and nothing else as far as he could see, it was hard to figure out what.

Inkerswell's cook had sloshed the back step with hot water to rid it of ice that morning, but the front of the house waited for a hint of sun to do the job. The cook said she'd get to it. She bustled through the doorway at the back and when she saw him, she told Inkerswell to mind the front step if he went out as she hadn't yet made it that far.

The front of the house had ice and snow still clinging to it when Mr Vernon and George struggled up the steps and along the path to the front door.

They knocked at the front door with anger bursting in their bodies.

"Gentlemen," Inkerswell said. "What can I do for you today?"

George's feet were unsteady on the icy path and Mr Vernon held the side of the door in case he also felt his shoes slip.

"Can we come in?" George said. "We have somert... important to talk to yer about."

Inkerswell stood aside to let the two men in. No sooner were they in the house than they started to talk.

"It's about Bradshaw," George said. "And what 'e's done to Sarah."

"Go on," Inkerswell said.

"Well...'e...'e's killed 'er."

Inkerswell could see by their eyes that this took up every moment of their waking hours, and that their sleeping ones weren't many. "That's quite an accusation," he said.

"Aye, well, we wun't be 'ere now telling you this if we din't know it's true."

"How do you know this?" he asked.

"Old woman Mattson, 'er lad told us. 'E saw it!"

Mr Inkerswell looked at the two men with an upturned gaze. He studied them a moment more. "He saw this?" he asked.

"'E sees things!" George said. "'E dun't mean 'e saw it, 'e means 'e saw it."

Mr Inkerswell kept his gaze on the two men while they waited for his response.

"'E showed us where," Mr Vernon put in. "'E took us out and 'e told us where Bradshaw's buried 'er."

"I see," Inkerswell said. "Well now, that is something."

*

Once this had come to Mr Inkerswell he felt his position weigh more on him than it had any other time yet. His house sat on a slight incline opposite the church and he would see the tower piercing the sky at any time he looked from his windows or from his place at the front door. He had a responsibility to the people who lived in this village. They were his, almost like they were the parson's. They needed him to keep peace and order and to protect them from malicious harm.

From his upstairs window he could almost see the graves in the churchyard opposite. Past relatives. His own, and those of the families now walking in the village. Mothers and fathers of those who drank in the Kingston Arms and sat quietly in the pews at church every Sunday. He owed it to all of them. Besides, he'd never liked Bradshaw.

*

In the cold, cracked and hard earth. At the back of Joseph's house. Under the spine-like branches of the coarse trees. Under the layer of snow. And then, melting away, still under icy patches that crunch when walked on like the shells of snails. In the ground, in the wet earth. Sarah still lies. No one comes. No one walks over her, stamping the brittle winter ground, or compacting it when it's softer and warmer and the ice is melting away. No one seems to know she is there. Although they do. Joseph, Anne, George and Mr Vernon, Aaron and Mr Inkerswell. All know she is there. But still no one comes.

Joseph cannot bear to walk up through the trees with Bess anymore. He recoils from the thought of treading on the ground Sarah lies beneath. He walks the edges of the fields instead. Late at night he walks to the outskirts of the village, and sometimes out by the stream, but mostly he keeps to the fields and he eyes the place up behind his house with something like suspicion, something like fear, as if Sarah might feel him there and claw her way out of the ground, her body grey, her hair gone, her heart set against him.

Anne keeps her face turned away from the trees and any thought of Sarah's body. As time passes, Anne finds she hates Sarah Vernon more and more. The girl brought trouble to Anne's house and if she'd lived who knows what she might have done. She was probably a witch. Certainly had the devil in her.

Mr Inkerswell told George and Mr Vernon not to go up to Bradshaw's land. He told them not to invite more trouble to their own households and to hold their nerve. He said to wait, not long, but to wait, and under no circumstances were they to confront the suspect.

Only Aaron had gone. Taking the path around the top field and standing up above on the horizon with the cattle that moved slow and groaned deep. Moving unseen through the few trees huddled together by the edge of the house. Waiting and listening and watching the place where Sarah was. Speaking quietly as he sent out a prayer for her poor soul. But the more he looked, darkness and the slow-moving cows on the horizon and the size and shape of the moon pulling him one way then the other, the less sure he was of the exact spot.

*

Aaron was sitting alone when George and Mr Vernon came to find him at the hovel. He was busy carving out shapes in thick pieces of wood. Not how his mother had shown him. He

86

wasn't scoring symbols into the flesh of the wood with the intention of altering folks' feelings and inclination. Aaron hadn't done much of that since his mother had died. He'd sat and he'd thought about it. But no one ever paid money for those talismans. No one saw the worth in them. They would take these things into their homes with utter belief, but they wanted it for free. Aaron had decided his future lay in carving wood for decoration. He had been sitting alone till the darkness of evening made it impossible to continue, and he had been carving animals and birds from blocks of soft wood. For those that wanted such things, he would attach a story of superstition and he would tell them what they wanted to hear. He found the two things worked well together, and the sight of such beautiful carvings made people sigh with delight. And they would pay.

This evening, Aaron was still busy with the wood on the floor of the hovel, though the light was fading fast, when there was a knock. He went to the door and felt his heart fall in his body when he saw who stood there.

"Yer to come with us," George said.

"Why?" Aaron asked.

"Inkerswell says. We're to go tonight. We meet 'im up by Bradshaw's place."

Aaron peered around George's body at Mr Vernon standing behind him. He held two shovels in his arm, his body leaning against them slightly.

"What is this?" Aaron asked.

"We're to find Sarah," George went on, "and you know where she is."

Aaron felt something pull heavy and deep in his middle. He closed his eyes, and when he opened them again George and Mr Vernon were still staring at him, waiting.

"Why would you disturb her?" he asked. "She sleeps quite peacefully."

He saw the sudden change in George's face, a redness blooming in his cheeks. "Sleeps peacefully? She deserves a proper burial."

"But I hardly think digging..."

Mr Vernon stepped forward. "She is my child. 'E killed 'er and I want 'im dead for this. We're going to find 'er to prove 'e did this, and you are coming with us."

Aaron looked down at Mr Vernon's finger pointing at his chest. The man was deadly serious and Aaron could see there was no way out of this. He sighed as he stepped out of his home and closed the door behind him.

They took the bottom road, winding up out of the village and towards the peak of the hill. They reached the lane and the bushes where Sarah had once waited. They walked by the drystone wall, low like a calf, where her life left her. And they walked without any hesitation onto Bradshaw's land, along the path which led to Bradshaw's front door, and by the house. From here they walked up alongside the fields, up where the trees lined the horizon like feathers, where the moon hung low and the wind filled every space. When they reached the slope where the branches touched and the leaves covered the ground, the three men met Inkerswell.

"Evenin'," he said. "'Tis a solemn business, sirs, but needs must."

Aaron looked down at the shovel Inkerswell also held.

"The three of us will dig, you will tell us where. I understand you do know where?"

Aaron looked at Inkerswell in the darkness. There was something in him Aaron couldn't fathom at first. George and Mr Vernon were filled with grief and emotions which couldn't find a direction. That was obvious and understandable, they both loved her, albeit in different ways. But Inkerswell... he was here for the law, of course, and something else.

Aaron began to make his way down the slope. "My sight is always sure," he answered, "but beyond that I cannot say."

"What the devil does that mean?" Inkerswell asked.

"Sir, I believe it is for each man to look inside themselves and find their own reasons for the things they do. I am not here to say."

"No, yer not," George called. "Yer 'ere to show us where 'e buried 'er."

88

Halfway into the trees Aaron stopped. The three men followed and stopped when he did.

"Here?" Inkerswell asked.

Aaron looked at him again. He was eager to do this. Eager to dig in the earth and find the poor girl's body. Too eager. Aaron breathed in deeply and looked around. Then he moved on without a word, the three men following him again, their shovels scraping the ground behind them.

They had moved on no more than six feet when Aaron stopped again.

"Here?" Inkerswell said.

Aaron looked at him in the darkness. He could feel the edge to the way he asked the question. He was impatient and becoming more annoyed with every step they took through the trees.

"I am sorry this is not as easy as you had hoped," Aaron answered.

"Don't fool with me," Inkerswell said. "Do you know the place or don't you?"

The anger came through in his words, and Aaron could see this was not about Sarah for him. It was about Bradshaw.

"I know that this happened," Aaron answered. "I saw it, but you must understand, the darkness and the trees, the way this land is, makes it difficult to know where."

George shoved his spade hard into the ground. "Yer said yer knew! Yer said she were 'ere!"

"She is here... somewhere. I said I knew he had buried her here, but the exact spot..."

Inkerswell looked at the other two men. "This is no use then," he said. "The girl could be anywhere, we'll never find her like this."

"What do we do?" George asked.

The three men seemed to disregard Aaron now he was no longer any use to them.

"We get him anyway," Inkerswell said. "We get Bradshaw."

*

The next evening the constable walked from the Kingston

Arms and up the hill. He walked with ale in his blood to aid his way. Up out of the Low Drop, his face, flushed against the cold air, turned slightly to meet the sleet that fell onto his skin. This was a bad business and truth be known, he hated being constable. Folk's faces when they saw him coming. Poor people who he knew felt desperate. Drunks, and men driven mad by women. Petty thieves who looked at him with loathing. There wasn't even any money in it. But he had no choice.

He walked up and out of the village, past the church and onto the road. There he couldn't see more than a dog's hind leg in front of him. The sleet was fast from the sky and filled the air like a swarm. He kept his face turned down into his collar as he walked. Up and around as the road bent, then dipped, then rose again all the way up to Bradshaw's farm. To the right somewhere was the stream, and the hovel where the lad Mattson lived. They said his mother had just since died, though no one seemed to know any details of it. It was Mattson, so Vernon and his neighbour said, who had "seen" all this. Just what truth there was in that the constable didn't rightly know, but that wasn't his business. Bradshaw was guilty, that's all he knew, that's all that mattered. And he was guilty. He had done something with the girl. Everyone knew that.

He reached the farm and he stopped for a moment. He'd much sooner have found Bradshaw in the village, even better in the Low Drop, but Bradshaw didn't show his face down there anymore, not since Sarah had gone.

He stood and looked over the fields, stretching up towards the sky, heaving in the cold, wet air. He couldn't see the man from here, so he decided to call at the house. Joseph wouldn't be there, but his wife probably would be. He walked along the path, the bushes busy around his legs. Once at the house he knocked on the door and breathed in his nervousness.

Anne answered. She looked him up and down and then settled her eyes on his. Waited. Didn't speak at all.

"Mrs Bradshaw," he said. "I wonder if yer know

where I might find yer 'usband."

Anne pushed her hands firmly down against her apron, as women do, and seemed to swallow hard.

"'E might be with his stock right now," she answered. "'Ere, I'll come out with yer and see."

She turned away back into the house and the constable put his hand out as if he was steadying her. "No, there's no need." He didn't want the man's wife along to witness this, but it was too late, she was back at the door and ready to step out into the thick sleet.

Anne walked ahead of the constable, to the right where the land stretched a little higher. The ground was still firm and edged with ice and snow, the low stone walls lined with it, ice nestled into every crack. Anne walked quickly and didn't speak. When they reached the cattle shed it was Bess who announced them, up on her feet fast and barking into the air at the constable. The constable looked warily down at the dog and then up and straight at Joseph.

"Joseph Bradshaw," he said.

"Aye" – though they both knew one another and there was no need for this. Just like they both knew why the constable was here. Joseph kept one hand on the cow nearest to him and waited. It felt like the seconds couldn't speak, like the moments were mute and blind and nothing could function anymore. It felt so long before the constable spoke again, but then after it would feel as if this had all happened too fast, like every second had tumbled over the next and the moments had rolled like barrels. Anne was waiting behind the constable, the two men facing each other.

"You are to be charged with murder, Bradshaw," the constable said.

Anne had known this was coming, had prepared herself, but still she found her hands covering her mouth and her breath sharp in her throat.

"You are to be charged with the murder of Sarah Vernon."

Today

"Are you free on Friday?"

She can hear him fumble with the phone, take a breath like a smoker and then say, "Friday? Well, I am kinda busy."

She sighs, and then remembers herself, remembers where she is and what she wants. She is a woman of small means who wants better. And she has seen a way she might get it. And at this point in the game she still needed to be charming.

"Can't you get out of it?" she asks. "Can't you put stuff off? I really want to see you."

She can hear the pull and fray in his breathing, can almost see what his face looks like at that moment. He's lilting so easily.

Ever since they went to that stupid hotel Lorraine has felt like she's two halves of the same issue. The story the woman from the hotel told her. That stupid night they'd spent in that stupid hotel. The noise in the night, the weird dream, *seeing* that girl. And she couldn't forget about it. Couldn't shake the thing. The thing that clung to her. That girl. Murdered by a man who, basically, let's face it, Lorraine thought, had his cake and ate it. Or in this case, killed it. Lorraine felt like it was following her, and she couldn't help but relate it to her own situation. Glenn had to pay. She wouldn't let him take what he wanted and then walk away leaving her with nothing. He had to pay.

"I'll make it worth your while," she says. She smiles to herself now, knows she's got him with that, knows Glenn can never turn away when she offers it to him like that.

"Well... I suppose I could. Just this once. What are you wearing?"

"Right now?"

"Yeah."

Lorraine looks down at herself in the kitchen. She's wearing an old pair of jeans and a T-shirt. She hasn't washed her hair today and hasn't bothered with make-up, no one was gonna see her anyway, except her husband.

"A tight T-shirt dress and red tights," she answers.

"Foxy. What about underneath?"

She smiles to herself. "Underneath I'm wearing the cream satin set you like."

"The low-cut one? The one that barely covers your nipples?"

"That's the one," she answers.

He was too easy. He really was too easy.

*

On Friday she waits for him to text her. He's pulled up down the road, around the street. She leaves the house and walks brazenly down to where he waits. She's wearing black jeans, knee-length boots and a tight sweater. Glenn looks at her as she approaches the car, opens the door and gets in.

"What, no T-shirt dress and red tights?" he asks with a smile.

"In this weather, you must be joking."

He leans over and pulls the neck of her sweater down. "What about underneath?"

"For God's sake, Glenn, get your hands off, at least wait till we're out of my neighbourhood."

He laughs and holds his palms up like he's been caught out. "OK," he says. "You're the boss. Where to?"

Lorraine looks straight ahead and sits upright. "I want to go back to that village we got lost in last week."

He just stares at her for a minute. "What? You mean the hotel?"

"No, not the hotel. I'm never going back there. The village."

"What do you want to go there for?"

She looks to her lap. Like a girl, he thinks, like she's no more than a girl.

"I just do," she says quietly. Then she looks up at him. "You'll think it's stupid. You'll think I'm stupid."

"No, I won't."

"You will."

He shrugs and looks at the road in front of him. He

puts his hand forward and turns the key in the ignition. "Well, maybe," he says. "But, OK, if that's what you want."

She thought it was strange how they'd got lost here before, taken a wrong turn or not taken a turn at all, and ended up driving down into the hollowed-out belly of this village. They'd chanced on this place by mistake. And now finding it again seemed so easy. Like it was... meant to be. But that was ridiculous. Lorraine didn't believe in any of that old crap. Destiny. Fate. Meant to be. Load of old bollocks.

Glen drove out towards the hotel. He drove past the turning and the long road that led up to the old building. Past those fields and the trees that slotted in beside it. He carried on, out along the road and then on to the village. It felt like there was no other way they could have gone. And maybe it was that simple, she thought. Maybe they found it again so easily because there were no other roads to take out here.

"You remembered the way," she said.

"Sort of," he replied. "I remembered generally where it was, though I don't think I'd ever been here before, but I remembered whereabouts it was. And then we were here."

Yeah," she said. And she looked at him while he drove. "That's what I thought. Then we were here, just like that."

"So, what do you want to do now?"

Lorraine could already feel his tone sinking. There was no sex imminent in his day and he was wondering what the point was. Why was he even here?

"Let's have a look round," she said. "Go for a walk."

"A walk?"

"Yes, Glenn, a walk, it's not that ridiculous. We can do other things apart from sex."

He looked sulky. "Didn't think you wanted to do other things," he said.

She ignored him while he found a place to park. She did want to do other things. He had that wrong. She wanted to do lots of things. She had a whole life ahead and she wanted to do so many things. But for that she needed money.

Glenn turned the car into a small, gravelly car park and

slowed to a standstill. "Here looks OK," he said. "For your walk."

They got out of the car and set off across the road. Just past the church there was a signpost and a path.

"Here," she said. She was walking ahead of him. He stopped and held his arms out from his body slightly, like he was inviting applause.

"Aw, what?" he said. "There's a pub back there, look, why don't we just..."

"Hang on," she answered. "In a bit. First I just want to..."

Lorraine walked slowly to a couple of cottages with house names on plaques on their walls, by their doors. Whatever it was that was bothering her lately, whatever she had seen in the mirror at the hotel and had heard in the night and had witnessed standing by the side of the road around this village, had begun here. Well, at the hotel, but it came from here, according to that woman at the hotel; so the story went anyway. She took a deep breath. She sounded like a madwoman. This was ridiculous. It was probably just the stress of her situation, what she was getting up to, the way she was living, all the sneaking around and lying and... she peered closer at the plaque on the wall. Here lived Sarah Vernon, whose fate...

"Gotcha!"

She jumped and turned fast. "Jesus, Glenn! Don't sneak up on me like that."

He grinned and put his arm around her. "Hey, the pub has rooms... or there's a nice bush over there, or we could always sneak into the church, no one would know."

She almost told him what a dog he was then, but she remembered herself.

"Let's go for that walk first," she said.

*

A small signpost and a stile marked the beginning of a track. A country walk. This path had been walked already by ramblers and day-trippers and school parties and Sunday plodders. The ground was mushy under their feet, the shallow heels of their boots sinking with every step.

"Bloody hell," she said, as the mud oozed around the leather and made tide lines. The snow was still patchy on the fields and from a distance it looked like a white crayon-rub on bumpy green paper. "Bloody stupid countryside."

Glenn laughed. "You were the one who wanted to come here."

She glared at him and held her hand out to a low branch to steady herself. "I thought it would be... beautiful," she said.

"Why would you think that?"

They were walking a path behind a row of bushes and trees, up out of the main part of the village.
"People are always saying how it's scenic and all that, aren't they?"

He walked behind her, putting his hand to his thigh, just above his knee, with every step. "Yeah, but you must have been out here as a kid or something."

She kept her face straight. "Not really," she said.

"Not at all?"

She stopped and looked out over the fields to the right. It was a strange kind of air out here. People always went on about the quiet, but it wasn't quiet, it was just a different noise. She could hear birds like she'd never heard them before. The far-off bark of a dog. Machinery. "No," she said.

"How come?"

"My mum didn't have time, and there wasn't really anyone else to bring me out here."

"So, that's why you wanted to come here today?"

She turned back to the path ahead of her. It dipped down and then up again and round a bend. Going down was harder than going up and her feet slid and her body felt like it would topple as her legs strained to deal with the ground.

"Something like that," she said.

Glenn stumbled a little behind her and fell against her shoulder. He put his hand out and held her arm, their bodies shunting.

"That's kinda sad," he said.

She turned and looked at his face. Saw a flicker of empathy.

"It is, isn't it?" she answered.

Then it was gone and he was looking at the path ahead of them.

"Come on," he said. And he patted her backside and pushed her forward.

She felt a change on the breeze. The air wasn't as cold down in the village, surrounded by the hills and houses and other buildings. Up here the air was empty and it spun around faster, trying desperately to find a place to settle. As they tackled the path leading up and around, out of the dip and into the bend, Lorraine could feel the wind circle her arms and legs and rush in her ears and through her hair. She turned her head slightly to Glenn walking behind her.

"The thing is," she said, "we never had any money, see, and Mum worked all the time and, well, I don't suppose she could have brought me out here if she'd wanted to."

She could feel him nod his head as he looked to the ground where his feet tried to find the brittle, snow-hardened patches of earth to walk on. "Aha."

"But mostly it was down to money – well, everything always is, isn't it?"

"I suppose."

They had made it up and around the bend. A stream ran to the left of the road and the fields stretched over the land like long, solemn breaths. They walked over towards the stream and Lorraine stood, hands on hips, and looked all around her. She could feel a strange mixture of fear and belonging, of this being the right time and the right place, but still somehow wrong.

"It is always about money, Glenn," she said. "Everything is always about money."

The words were trickling from her like the stream through cracks in the rocks and springing from the earth in places.

"Not everything," he replied. "Not always."

"That's easy for you to say. You've got money. It's always easy to say that when you've got money."

She could feel a frown tightening on his face, but she didn't look at him. She was looking all around her, at the place she stood in. A stream and the arch of a field like a bent back. The sky heavy and the clouds rolling. It was a feeling, just a feeling.

"What's got into you?" he asked. "You do alright. I see you do alright."

It was a feeling. Then a realisation. The fields and the sky and the stream and the hill. She was standing in the same place she'd seen in that picture at the hotel. Or one of those pictures anyway. Not the one with the weird-looking creepy man holding his vessel up to the air, doing his thing, but one of the other landscape ones. She was sure of it. She was standing in the exact same place right now. She smiled to herself. It was a sign. A bloody sign. Lorraine didn't believe in signs or any of that crap, but this was a sign. This was meant to happen. She was on the right track. She couldn't miss with this. She had history and signs and bloody ghosts on her side.

She turned and looked Glenn right in the eyes. He was still frowning, and he saw the harshness take hold of her and fix itself under her skin. And he thought he didn't really know her at all then.

A half-smile opened at one side of her mouth. She felt a ghost in her. The ghost of a girl done wrong by a greedy dog of a man. That wouldn't happen to Lorraine.

"I do alright," she said. "But Julia does better."

Derbyshire, 1760s

"I can read."

    "Can yer, now?"

    "Aye, I can."

    The constable blew out a laugh and pushed Joseph forward, up the path of the large house Inkerswell lived in, towards the door. He didn't try to hide his contempt and disbelief at what Joseph had just said. They stood at the door while they waited for it to be opened and they both looked ahead. Joseph turned slightly to check the constable's face.

    "I mean it," he said. "I can read."

    The constable eyed him from the corner of his vision. "Aye, well," he answered, "we'll see about that."

    Inkerswell's cook was the one who opened the door, standing there and clearly looking Joseph up and down like he was cattle to be bought. She pushed one hand down on her apron and with the other she pulled the door open wider. "Right," she said. "Let's 'ave yer in, then."

    The constable brought Joseph to a room. The window in front of him as he entered looked over the gardens. Gardens the likes of, Joseph had never seen. The snow was piled on the branches of trees and covered the ground everywhere still but, beyond and beneath, Joseph could see flowers growing in ordered bushes and he knew the grass was clipped and organised like a piece of furniture. Joseph looked out at the paper-white sky and the neat, peaceful grounds, and felt he was already imprisoned.

    In front of him Inkerswell sat at a dark wood table the size of a bed.

    "This is Joseph Bradshaw," the constable said, although they all knew exactly who one another were. Inkerswell nodded and looked down at the papers on the table. "Charged with the murder of Sarah Vernon," the constable went on. "Sez 'e can read."

    Mr Inkerswell looked up sharply. He stared into Joseph Bradshaw's face. Bradshaw's eyes avoided his stare and fixed on the window behind him instead. The man was tall, broad-shouldered, good-looking; Inkerswell supposed that's why he was in this trouble. Woman had seen all that Inkerswell could see and it had meant more to her than it should have. Bradshaw was physically strong. He was quick-tempered and arrogant. Popular with some of the men in the Kingston Arms, and not with others. He was hardy. Nothing he didn't know about the land and how to work it. He wasn't literate. Inkerswell was as sure of that as he could be.

"You can read?" Inkerswell asked, his doubt plain in his face and his question.

Joseph still avoided looking at him. "Aye," he said, "that I can."

Inkerswell tapped the edge of the table with his finger and looked down at the papers again. "Hmm," he said. "Well, now, that is unexpected. I should think, with that in mind, you'll be wanting to claim benefit of clergy."

"Aye," Joseph answered.

Inkerswell eyed the man. Standing tall, his shoulders back, staring out of the window, his clear blue eyes searching the garden outside. He was perfectly entitled to this, no matter what Inkerswell thought.

He nodded to the constable. "Very well," he said.

*

Joseph had barked louder and angrier than Bess when he was taken that morning. Anne knew he could see her crumbling and she knew he hated it. Anne had felt a fear and a sickness take hold of her skin and all that lay beneath it, as she watched the constable give her husband the news they knew was coming.

"I'll come," she'd said, feebly. And she'd looked around her as if there was some help to be found in the snow-covered ground or in the footprints left by her and the constable, or in the cold, blank sky.

"No!" Joseph had shouted then. She'd looked at him, but his face was harsh and cold like the air. "You stay 'ere," he'd said, "with Bess."

Anne looked down at the dog. Her ears had flattened

against her head and her body cowed against the terrible feeling of fear and separation. She wagged her tail in hope for a moment and nosed Joseph's leg. Anne felt the weight of feeling between the man and this animal like a stone. It took Anne's breath from her throat and made her feel like she couldn't breathe. She thought she saw the sadness in Joseph's eyes then, as he had to walk away from Bess. The dog tried to follow and Joseph shouted "Getcha!" and pointed away from him. The dog whimpered and leaned herself against the cold air and away from Joseph. Anne didn't go to the dog then, but just stood stranded in the field as the constable walked away with Joseph. When the two men had left more footprints in the brittle icy snow that covered the land than she could count, Anne went to the dog and put her arms around the animal. Bess licked Anne's face quickly and lifted her paws to Anne's bended knees. They walked back to the house together.

Today

"What did you mean by that?"

Lorraine stood with her hands on her hips, on an incline, on slightly higher ground, looking down on Glenn. "What?" she said.

"What you just said, about Julia, what's that supposed to mean?"

Lorraine shrugged and looked to the side, over the fields. "Just an observation," she said.

"Since when did you make 'observations'?"

She looked at him sharply. "Oh, I make observations, Glenn," she said. "Don't you worry about that."

Glenn put a hand to his thigh, just above his knee, and leaned on it. "Jeesh, Lorraine, come on, what's wrong with you? You know the deal. You know how it is. Julia is... separate. You know that. It's a separate issue. You know she'd ruin me if she found out. It would be the end of me."

"Yeah, well, sometimes..."

Glenn took a step forward and reached out to her arm. "Come on, babe," he said. "Don't be like this. We've got the whole day together. We could go down to that pub, get a room."

Was that all he ever thought about? Was that all it was, really? Didn't the way she felt or what she wanted out of life matter to him at all? She had the sudden sense of being used. He kept his comfortable home life and his money and he got to have Lorraine when he wanted as well. She had the sudden feeling of not being in control. He was using her. He thought he had it all. He thought he could have what he wanted when he wanted it. And, in the end, why should she mind? It was only sex. She didn't care. She'd get what she wanted in the bargain. She'd get more than he realised yet. She would.

Glenn was standing right by her now, one arm snaking round her waist. "It's just you and me," he said. "You know I love it when it's just you and me."

She'd planned on doing it right now, here, where there was no one around. Where he couldn't get away from it, make excuses, wriggle his way out. But she hadn't done it. And now she was looking at him and he was calling her "babe" and saying these things... She could feel the moment slipping away. She'd bottled it. She knew the moment had gone. She was going to do it and then he'd said that thing about how Julia would ruin him and it would be the end of him, and he'd looked at her with that puppy expression, like he was so bloody vulnerable. Really. Glenn, vulnerable, it was stupid, it was laughable. And then he'd followed it up by making her feel he wanted her. How did he do it?

She took a sidelong look at him and felt a smile creeping on her face. The strange thing was, she knew he was using her, but he still got her with it. It was in the way he said things and the look on his face and the promise of how he'd make her feel. Lorraine couldn't fathom it. She knew what was going on. Yet she couldn't resist him. She really didn't know how he did it sometimes. He was such a dog, and yet he always got her. She didn't care. She really didn't care, but it was like he could persuade her out of her clothes with no more than a look.

"Oh yeah?" she said.

"Yeah, baby." And he leaned forward and began kissing her. She let him for a minute, then she pushed him away and thumped his shoulder.

"Alright then," she said. "Take me to the pub then and buy me champagne."

"Cham-bloody-pagne?"

She still had her hand in a fist on his shoulder and she leaned her face away from him now. "Aren't I worth it?" she asked.

"You'd bloody better be," he answered. "You'd better be worth it for at least three hours."

*

She tried to stop at the cottage with the plaque on the outside again, but Glenn was holding her hand and he led her on, eager to get to the pub.

The pub stood right on the edge of the road and looked

like it was only the size of a modest house. Lorraine stared up at the stone walls as Glenn pushed the door. A sign said "Mind the step" and they both looked down as they entered. They stepped down into the pub and walked straight up to the bar.

"You got any champagne, mate?" Glenn asked the barman.

The barman raised an eyebrow and drew breath in tightly. He bent to a fridge behind the bar and brought out a bottle. "Yeah, sure," he said. "You celebrating?"

Glenn leaned on the bar. "Yeah, something like that. You do rooms, don't you?"

The barman held his hands tightly around the end of the bottle and made a stern expression as he worked the cork free. It popped and a vapour like a whisper escaped slowly. He sat the bottle down and brought two glasses onto the bar. "Well, aye, normally we do," he said. "But right now they're being done up, so no."

Glenn and Lorraine exchanged a glance and the barman watched them. He turned away and fetched a cooler, then slid the bottle inside. "Only other place you'll get a room is up at the hotel," he said. "I can give you directions if you like."

Glenn looked at the champagne bottle. "Can we walk to it?"

"Yeah, easy," the barman answered. And he leaned on the bar towards Glenn.

Lorraine touched Glenn's arm. "Just gonna find the loo," she said.

"Straight through there, love," the barman shouted.

Lorraine followed his arm and saw the sign for the toilets.

Inside a cubicle, she sat down and breathed deeply. She had this. She was in control. She knew what she was going to do and she had it covered. Bloody men. All of them worth bugger all. Might as well get what she could out of them. She could carry this off, she knew she could. She was strong. She was tough. She had to survive, after all. She had to

104

live.

She looked up at the door of the cubicle she sat in. Someone had taped a piece of paper up on the door that said "Please unlock the door before trying to open it". How ridiculous was that? Seriously, it must be true what they say about villagers. Bloody nut jobs. Who would try opening a door without unlocking it? And why was there a need for a sign to say so?

She stood up again when she'd finished and turned around to flush the toilet. There was a small window behind her, open a little, and a cold winter breeze blew suddenly in, ruffling her hair. She turned back to the door and pulled at the lock. It was stuck. She looked up at the paper taped on the door and she let go a small laugh. This was ridiculous. She pulled at the lock again, but it wouldn't budge. She pulled and pushed it faster, stood still a minute to catch her breath, then tried again, moving it up and down and from side to side, getting anxious. But she couldn't shift it. The wind blew in again behind her and her hair lifted. Lorraine felt the coldness on the back of her neck where her hair was moved away from her skin. Then something else. Something touching her. She instinctively flapped her hair with one hand while she frantically pulled at the lock with the other. "Hey," she shouted. "Hey, I'm stuck." The wind blew once more in through the window and Lorraine felt a touch on her neck, light and as dainty as gentle fingers. She shrieked and looked around. The open window only showed a small slice of the outside, but right there Lorraine saw a trail of brown hair move as though belonging to someone half-running.

She turned back to the door, pressing herself against it and desperately trying to move the lock. "Help!" she shouted. "Get me out!"

The door was flung open and there stood the barman.

"Didn't you read the sign?" he asked, pointing to the paper taped onto the door. "It's a tricky lock, you have to lift it, but there's no use rattling the door like that."

Lorraine stared at him. She realised her breathing was heavy and she must have looked scared. He stared back at her.

"Well, it does say," he said, motioning to the sign again.

Lorraine pushed past him and back out into the bar. She sat down opposite Glenn and downed the glass of champagne he'd poured her, then instantly poured herself another.

"Since there's no rooms here," he said, absently, "we'll have to go to the hotel. Don't worry, I got directions. Looks like it's back up were we've just been walking. So you get to walk it again now."

He smiled at her and leaned forward and squeezed her knee. She looked at him, downed the champagne and poured more.

*

After four glasses straight, Lorraine felt her heart slow and her blood run easier in her veins. Glenn wasn't getting much of the champagne but she needed it more, and, besides, he'd have to drive later.

He motioned to her glass still held firmly in her hand. "You're going it a bit, aren't you?" he said.

She looked away from him. There were pictures on the wall in this pub not unlike the ones in that hotel, though not the same, of course, she thought.

"Yeah, well, you'll have to drive later, anyway, so it's better if I drink it."

She didn't look at him but carried on scanning the wall. Some of the pictures in this pub were done by local artists. A handwritten sign, painted in swirly writing, offered them for sale at £25 each, the artist's name alongside with the word "local" shining on the notice especially for tourists. Beside these were a couple of dark pictures like the ones Lorraine had seen on the wall at the hotel. She tried to look more closely at them but found her vision wouldn't play.

"Actually," Glenn said, "I was thinking we could stay over, if you can swing it."

She turned to him. "What?"

"Call your husband," he said. "I'll make up some story for Julia."

Lorraine narrowed her eyes at him. "Why?" she asked. "Why do you want to do that?"

He shrugged. "Just want to. You know I love sleeping with you."

Lorraine peered at him, then turned back to the pictures on the wall. "I know you like being in bed with me," she muttered. "Different thing."

She could feel Glenn shift in his chair as she stared up at the wall again. He was put out by that thing she just said. Stupid. Why would he be bothered, and, anyway, it was true, wasn't it?

That girl. The one who'd lived here in this village. The one who'd obviously got under Lorraine's skin somehow, wormed into her brain and now she was going half-crazy thinking she was seeing her... ghost or something stupid. That girl. She'd let herself be taken for a fool. She'd let a man have his way and give her nothing in return. She'd been stupid, and look what happened to her. It was extreme, yeah, but still... the way Lorraine saw it, you either get wise where men are concerned or they walk all over you.

She was still looking up at the pictures when she saw one like the one in the hotel. Dark. Almost as if it was rubbed over in coal. Showing the same house on a hill, but no one in the foreground of this one. Just the house. No people in this picture.

The barman was stooping over the table then and Glenn was shunting in his chair. The barman lifted up the champagne bottle, shook it to check it was empty, then picked up the cooler with the bottle in to take it away. Lorraine turned around. "Hey," she said. "This picture, here."

The barman glanced up.

"Where is this house?" Lorraine asked.

The barman straightened to a standing position and looked at the picture. "Hill Head House," he said. "No, it's not there anymore."

"Well, what happened to it?"

The barman shrugged and picked up the two glasses from the table like he was running sand through his fingers. "I don't know," he said. "Pulled down, I suppose."

He turned to walk away, but Lorraine stood up and carried on talking. "Pulled down?" she asked. "Because of what happened there?"

The barman stopped and looked at Lorraine, a smile settling in his face. "That's just a story, love," he said.

Glenn was tugging at her sleeve now. "Sit down," he said. "What are you going on about?"

She pushed his hand away, but still followed the barman with her eyes. "Did you see how he fobbed me off then?" she asked Glenn.

"Eh? Fobbed you off about what?"

"The house."

Glenn glanced from Lorraine to the barman. "What happened in the toilets, anyway?" he asked.

*

Lorraine was marching forward, out of the pub and along the lane, booze in her body, annoyed with the way these men were talking to her, treating her like some sort of idiot. "I'm telling you, Glenn," she said. "There's something going on here. He knows it." She stopped and pointed harshly back towards the pub.

Glenn tried to catch her arm but she pulled away from him. "What are you talking about? What the hell happened back there?"

She took a deep breath and lowered her voice a little. "I got locked in the loo, right," she said. "There's a sign on the back of the door, sez make sure you unlock the door before trying to open it, or something stupid."

He laughed.

"Yeah, I know," she said. "But I couldn't unlock the bloody door, and..."

She looked at him. He was going to think this was so stupid. He was going to tell her she was mad.

"And the window was open behind me and I... felt something."

She saw him frown, a curl of wariness roam in his

cheeks and above his eyes.

"And then... I saw someone outside, I think... I saw a girl's hair, like she was going past the window."

"So?" he asked.

"So, then the barman opened the door and made out like it was my fault, like I hadn't unlocked it first, I mean how stupid..." she was raising her voice again, the alcohol running again.

"Lorraine, you're not making any sense. Did he try it on with you in there?"

She stared hard at him. "What? Haven't you been listening?"

"Yeah, but seriously, all I'm getting is, you got stuck in the loo, that bloke went in there and got you out, two of you alone in the loos and then you're pissed off with him."

She stared at him a moment longer, then turned away. "Oh, for God's sake, Glenn!"

There was a couple at the other side of the lane, walkers by the looks of it, in their fifties, heavy boots to crush the snow and ice, raincoats ready for a downpour. They stood and gazed at this couple arguing in the quiet lane. Lorraine had a second of seeing herself how they must see her. They probably thought she and Glenn were married, or at least "together". They probably thought this was a mundane argument about the cold and the pub, or being lost, or even falling out of love. They'd never guess the grim truth. She held her arms out like she was inviting applause. "What are you looking at?" she shouted. The older couple looked faintly shocked or disgusted, turned to each other, then walked on, tutting under their breaths.

"Lorraine!" Glenn was moving slowly behind her, but Lorraine walked forward, towards the short row of cottages. "Lorraine, what the hell is wrong with you?"

He caught her up at the cottage with the plaque on the wall by the door. *Here lived Sarah Vernon.*

"This!" she said. "This is what is wrong with me. This girl, look!"

Glenn leaned forward and read the plaque. "Whose life

was cruelly taken," he read. He stood up straight and shook his head. "I don't get it."

"She's haunting me!"

Glenn shook his head again and let go a nervous laugh. "Nobody is haunting you, Lorraine, there's no such thing as... ghosts. Surely you don't believe..."

"Then how else do you explain all the stuff I've been seeing and hearing and... feeling?"

She could see his patience slip again. "I don't know!" he said. "Maybe you're tired, or stressed, or going mental, I don't know, but it's not a bleeding ghost!"

She let her body fall to one side, shoulder down, and took her top teeth behind her bottom, her jaw skewed. Glenn could see tears or anger or something else moving under her skin. Something aimed at him.

He drew breath in. Suddenly wondered what she might be capable of. Suddenly felt a flick of worry about getting on the wrong side of this woman. She knew all about Julia. She knew how to hurt him. "Look," he said. "I wasn't having a go, just think you're getting yourself worked up over nothing. Surely you don't think..."

He watched. Her expression stayed the same.

"Well, say you're right..." He flapped his arms out in frustration. Couldn't believe he was saying this. "What can we do?" He motioned to the plaque on the wall in front of them. "I mean... why would this girl be haunting you anyway?"

A Bad Winter

Derbyshire, 1760s

Anne woke to a bare window and a clear sky. The weather was slowly drawing back and the fresh morning breathed like new skin beneath a wound. Anne turned her head and upper body in the wide bed and felt the bulk of a living thing wedged behind her curved knees. Bess stayed in that position for a few more minutes and Anne was left uncomfortably still, not wanting to disturb the dog and not wanting to move away from her, so comforting was her warmth.

She could see the blue sky, white clouds pulled over it like cobwebs over beams, and the far off tops of hills as still as she was now. It seemed wrong that the day should start so clear and fresh, when her own world seemed to have ground to a halt. The season appeared to be shifting and getting ready to move on, but Anne couldn't see how that could be. It was still winter for her.

Eventually Bess moved, waking with Anne and shifting by her legs. She scrambled to her feet and stepped over Anne's body. Then she came to sit by Anne's side. Anne lifted her arm and stroked the dog's head and ears. Bess lifted her nose to nudge the air, then she dipped her head and began licking Anne's hand. Anne lay there watching the dog as she meticulously covered every inch of Anne's skin, cleaning in between her fingers and then right up to the tips of them.

She felt a tightening of a bond she'd not previously known was there, and the feeling of being cared for, the like of which she hadn't felt since she'd left her mother's house. Anne continued to watch, fascinated, as the dog cleaned her, totally focussed on this one act. Under the covers, Anne put her other hand to her stomach. She felt a sharp, glass-like pain down the side of her belly, right down towards the place where her tuft of hair began. She looked into the dog's eyes. A frown fluttered on Anne's face and a worry about a baby not yet known of dropped in her middle.

*

Anne had never taken the dog out on her own before. She

111

looked at the animal's sad eyes as she sat, back straight, nose up, tail trying desperately to be still, waiting for Anne to show the way. The poor thing, Anne thought. The poor, innocent thing.

They had got out of bed together as if they were bonded now, a couple, not to be separated. They had walked down the narrow staircase together and Bess had waited patiently while Anne made breakfast for them both, like they had always lived this way.

Then, when all was done in the kitchen, Anne had fetched her coat. That was when Bess had sat like this waiting. Eagerness to be out in the fields fighting inside her, struggling with the memory that she had to be still, had to wait, had to be patient. Joseph had always kept an obedient dog, and Bess had learned well not to overstep the mark.

She sat, alert to Anne's every movement, and Anne sighed as she looked down on Bess. She was going to have to take the dog with her. She'd never done this before, but there didn't seem to be another way now.

"You shall 'ave to come with me, girl," she said, and she wagged her finger at the dog in warning. "Mind you behave, though. Don't go giving me any trouble."

Outside, the air seemed different. The ground was still thick with snow and ice, though no more had fallen for a couple of days now. It was still bitterly cold, but something felt cleared. Like a fog lifted. Anne looked up at the clear, blue sky and thought that was where the change was. It was from above, she thought, as all things are.

She walked up, away from the house and the village, the rocky, icy path taking her higher into the clear air. Bess by her side, her spindly legs switching fast as she walked.

They walked together over the tops of the hills, Bess stopping every now and then to sniff the rocks or a patch of ground. Anne would wait for her, not sure how she should be called on.

After a little longer than Anne usually took on her own, she and Bess arrived at her mother and father's house. They walked together to the door and Anne stopped and looked down at Bess. "Now, yer can't come in, you 'ear?"

She looked down at the dog's mournful eyes, questions in the movements of her ears.

"You stay 'ere," she said.

Anne opened the door and walked in, leaving the dog staring after her.

*

"What a to-do," her mother said. She shook her head and blew air out through a strained mouth. "What a business."

"'E will get off though, won't 'e? 'E will..."

Anne's mother shifted her head from side to side as if weighing it on her shoulders. "I can't rightly say," she answered. "If it were drunkenness or even thieving... but murder... You'll 'ave to pray 'e does, Anne, we'll all 'ave to, or goodness knows what..."

Anne looked into her own lap. She felt responsible and guilty in front of her mother with this news, as if it was her fault. She supposed everyone would think it was in some way. Maybe they would be right. Maybe it was her fault. Maybe she'd driven him to this by being a bad wife, or neglectful, or just not enough for him. There had to be some reason Joseph felt the need to seek out Sarah Vernon. Maybe Anne should have been giving him whatever it was Sarah gave him.

Her mother reached forward and patted her hand. "Now then, Anne," she said. "Whatever 'appens will 'appen."

Anne looked up at her mother. There were tears in her eyes and she was fighting to keep them where they were. "There's something else," she said.

"And what's that?"

"When I last saw yer, mother, I told yer I may be 'aving a child."

Her mother sat back in her chair and lifted her chin. "Aye, yer did. And are yer?"

"Well, that's the thing. 'Ow would I know?"

Her mother shrugged. "Different ways. Yer mayn't bleed. Some bring their food up. Some just get fatter."

Anne stared away to the side for a moment. She couldn't comment on any of those things. Nothing like that had happened to Anne. "What about pain?" she asked.

"What sort of pain?"

"Just this morning I 'ad pain down 'ere." She put her hand to one side of her belly. "And it seemed to travel downwards... to..."

Her mother raised an eyebrow. "Aye well, girl, if Joseph 'as 'ad 'is way before 'e got taken, that may well be the thing right there. Only time can show that and yer'll 'ave to wait to gain an answer."

*

When Anne left the house she felt the confusion moving inside her. There didn't seem to be any straight answers to anything.

She opened the door and stepped out. Bess had been lying there waiting all along, laid beside the step as if guarding the house, or at least Anne. Anne felt a sudden fondness for the dog she never thought she'd feel. Bess got to her feet as soon as Anne stepped out and they walked away from the old house together.

Today

Lorraine thought she'd feel something, standing here in front of the cottage. She thought, if it was this girl, if this was the girl who the stories were about and who she kept seeing and hearing and feeling, she'd know it now. But she didn't feel anything. She wondered if it could be possible that there was another, but she knew it couldn't be. This was the girl. So, why did she see her up on the road and in the hotel and down in the pub? Why did she feel her and see her everywhere but here, at the girl's own house?

She thought about the story the older woman at the hotel had told her. A crazy story. She'd almost laughed when she'd heard it. Ridiculous the things people used to believe. But then... if you'd told Lorraine a month ago she'd be seeing ghosts she'd have laughed in your face about that too. And now look at me, she thought.

Glenn had walked a couple of paces away from her to phone Julia. Lorraine wasn't supposed to be in earshot of Julia. Glenn was always very insistent about this. The mere suggestion of it sent a shooting of anxiety through his body. Lorraine thought it was quite funny really.

She sidled up to him on purpose now, wanting to annoy him. She folded her arms around his. He pulled away. "I'm sorry, Ju," he was saying, "but it really is something I can't get out of. You know how it is with work at the moment."

Lorraine stared at him. Really, she had no idea why it rankled with her. It wasn't as if she didn't do her fair share of lying herself, but, somehow, the fact that Glenn was bare-faced lying right there in front of her bothered her. Stupid. Why should she care? And really, what did she expect? What else was he going to say?

He turned away from Lorraine. "Exactly, we can't afford to not follow up on all leads, even if they come to nothing. Way things are, I just don't think we've got a choice."

Wow. Poor cow. Lorraine actually felt sorry for her

now.

"No, I'll make sure it's not a late one, and I'll see you when I get back tomorrow."

Lorraine faced the cottage again while Glenn said goodbye, then she turned around and looked at him, her head cocked to one side.

"Impressive," she said. "You're a really good liar."

"What's that supposed to mean?"

She shrugged. "Nothing," she said. "Just, didn't realise you were such a natural at it."

"Well, what do you expect? What do you want me to say? Sorry, Julia, but I'll be shagging my bit on the side tonight?"

She turned her head as if he'd slapped her. "Bit on the side?"

"You know what I mean."

"Oh yeah," she said. "I know what you mean."

"Come on, Lorraine, don't tell me you're not gonna phone your husband right now and lie like I just did, because you know you are."

"And what if I didn't?"

"What do you mean?"

"What if I told him exactly where I am and what I'm doing?"

He stared at her. "Why would you do that?"

She turned away from him again and looked around her at the cottages. "Doesn't matter," she muttered. Then she turned back and faced him. "You know he knows about you, don't you?"

It was almost worth it for the look on his face.

"What?"

Lorraine suppressed a smile as she began walking away, towards the same walk they'd done earlier, away from the village, by the trees. Glenn caught her up and grabbed her arm. "What do you mean, he knows? You mean he knows about us?"

She shook him off and walked on. "He knows who you are. He knows we're friends."

116

"You told him?"

She was still moving ahead in front of him. She turned her head slightly to answer, holding the spindly branch of a tree as she passed it. "Yeah, well, I'm not as comfortable lying as you are, so I told him me and you are friends. That way I don't have to lie."

"I can't believe this," he said. "You actually told him. And does he know about...?"

Lorraine turned around in time to see Glenn make an over-exaggerated expression with his face.

"No, don't be stupid. I don't think that would go down too well, do you?"

"No, suppose not," he said. He moved his head around, mocking how she might have told her husband everything. "'Oh, by the way, we've had sex, quite a lot of it actually'."

She carried on walking, the icy ground slippery under her feet, the cold air stinging her ears. Glenn probably liked the idea on some level. It probably turned him on, imagining her husband finding out, imagining being the one who was "having" her instead of him. She could feel her power growing as she walked. Glenn had nothing on her. He couldn't do anything. He couldn't hurt her. Anything that got back to her husband could be explained away because she'd already told him about Glenn. She'd told him they were friends, so anything else could be explained away with that.

She trudged forward. She was going faster than earlier. Maybe because she was familiar with the way now. Maybe because she could feel all her nervous energy coming together and leading her on.

"What about Julia?" she said.

"What about her?"

"What if she found out?"

"About you and me? That's not even funny."

Lorraine smiled to herself. She had him. She could taste the fear in the air as his words came out sharp in the cold day.

"Yeah," she said. "I bet you'd do anything to make

sure that didn't happen."

She took a few more steps forward.

"Where did that guy say the hotel is?" she asked. She couldn't look at him. Knew her previous words were still roaming around in his brain. She could almost feel his stare and his slight frown.

"Bit further on," he said, quietly. "Then we cross the road."

"Right." She walked forward until she came to the road. Once there, she turned and slipped her hand into Glenn's. She even looked up at him and smiled. Like nothing had happened. But it was there. A dangerous silence breathing between them for a few minutes. They crossed the road together, the black runner of tarmac like an outstretched leg, leading up and over the top of the hill. On the other side of the road they walked until they saw the building rise in the sky in front of them.

"I don't believe it," he said. "It's the same bloody hotel."

*

He was quiet while he checked in. Lorraine was hovering over the pictures on the wall again, staring at the darkened one with the people gathered in front of the house. She turned in time to see Glenn offer the girl behind the desk a thin, resigned sort of smile. She felt a brief flutter of regret. She'd bothered him this time. She'd maybe gone too far, said too much, but he deserved it. He did deserve it.

She turned back to the pictures and Glenn came and stood by her side. "I'm gonna walk back down and fetch the car," he said. "Would have bloody driven up if I'd known." She didn't answer or look at him. The discomfort squirmed in her middle. Things had never been so... wrung between them. It had always been casual and light and... frivolous. It was her fault. No, she thought, it was his fault.

He moved to walk away, then held out the room key for her to take. "Did you really tell him about me?" he asked.

She looked up at him. "Yeah."

"But wouldn't he have been suspicious? Weren't you

worried?"

"No. Dunno. But either way, what do I have to worry about? He can't do much. It's not like you with Julia. We don't have any money, we don't have anything. "

He smarted slightly at her use of his wife's name. Then her words seemed to finger the flesh on his face, making him paler, drawn with a nagging fear. "Are you gonna call him?" he asked.

"Yeah, in a minute."

She looked up into his face. Almost felt sorry for him. Almost.

"Well... don't do anything hasty," he said. "I mean... don't..."

She smiled up at him. "Don't worry," she said. "You won't come into it. I'll tell him something else this time."

She let it hang there. Could feel him still glancing at her as he walked away to the door. Poor bastard. He had no idea what was going on.

She carried on gazing at the pictures, then took her phone from her pocket and called her husband's. She knew he wouldn't answer. Knew he'd be tied to his office desk at this time. She waited for the answering machine to click, the tone dull and forlorn, then she spoke hurriedly into the phone. "Hey, it's me, I've got something on tonight. See you tomorrow." She finished the call and shoved the handset back into her pocket. Men were unfathomable sometimes. And they say women are complicated. It seemed like the worse she treated him the more desperate to please her he became. It wasn't a bad thing. She got her way. But why he allowed her to carry on like this was beyond her. She was sure he knew what she was up to. How could he not? But he let it happen. And then there was Glenn. He thought he was in charge here. Thought he had a lid on this. Thought he could have his way and nothing would happen. She looked around her at the old, beautiful hotel where he expected to have just what he wanted when he wanted. He thought wrong.

She felt someone standing close to her then. A presence. She almost didn't dare to look. This place was haunted. This whole bloody village was haunted. She was haunted.

"I see you're still interested in our history," a voice said. Lorraine turned quickly and there was the older woman who'd told her the story the last time she was here.

"Oh, yeah," Lorraine answered. "I am, yeah."

The woman smiled. Her face was heavily wrinkled and covered in foundation and powder a shade lighter than her natural skin colour. Her eyes were made up in shades of brown, her lips red and her hair evenly dyed and set in soft waves. Lorraine wondered what she thought when she looked at Lorraine. Probably saw a slapper. Probably looked at the tight jeans and the knee-high boots, the black hair extensions and the close-fitting top, and presumed she was a common tart. Well, Lorraine thought, she'd be right. Why pretend otherwise?

"If you like, I can show you the outside of the building," she said.

Lorraine's face fell a little in confusion. The woman was already walking to the door and Lorraine followed her. She turned to speak as she passed through the door, holding it open for Lorraine to follow.

"This hotel was built on the exact spot, as far as we know." The woman smiled as she walked around to the left of the hotel. There was a car park both at the front and the back of the building, and the corner they stood on together now delivered a fantastic view over the fields and down towards the village, though you couldn't see it from up here. The road bent and dipped down there and trees and bushes lined the fields on the way down to the village, so all you could see from up here was sky and endless green.

"I'm sorry," Lorraine said, "I don't follow."

"The house," the woman said. "This is where the house was. Hill Head House. I'm afraid I don't know what happened to it, but this is where it was, right here." The woman pointed to the ground they were standing on, then she raised her arm and pointed up to the wooded area behind the hotel. "The story goes that she was buried in those woods up there," she went on, "the girl who was murdered." She dipped her head and said that last word in a hushed, over-dramatic way. "But I don't know how true that is. Anyway, we have some lovely woodland walks going through there now, and we even have a climbing wall, you know, for when the team-building lot come. We get a fair few of those."

Lorraine was staring around her. "So, this is where... and that picture you have on the wall in here, this is where..."

The woman smiled and nodded. Then she lowered her voice and her head again, as if she were a conspirator. "And that story I told you, the local legend – well, down there, you can see the stream. It's a nice walk. Worth a look."

Lorraine followed the woman's gaze. The fields tumbled down towards the village, and off to the right, where the road bent and dipped, the woman was directing Lorraine's eyes to where the water ran.

"The stream runs all the way along, you see," the woman said, "down there, so you can easily walk down the hill to it from here."

Lorraine felt a strange burn of something in her middle. Something like excitement and fear and nervousness and impatience. All expanding inside her. She thought about how cold the water would be in winter. How moments in icy water could kill a person. She thought about how it only takes inches of water to kill someone. A fresh breeze drifted down from the trees behind the hotel and blew the hair of Lorraine and the woman she stood with. Her coarse, black strands rose and touched the soft honey of the other woman and they both instinctively put their hands up to calm it. Lorraine would always feel there was something in the wind here now. Couldn't help it. She would always feel the delicate fingers of a girl moving in circles on her neck when her hair was lifted from it like that. She shuddered.

"Well, I'd better get back in," the woman said. "And here's your husband now."

Lorraine looked to her right, alarmed for the merest second. Then she saw Glenn's car pulling into the car park in front of the hotel.

Derbyshire, 1760s

"If you would like to read the passage which has been prepared from the bible in front of you..."

Joseph could feel a strange itch on his skin. He swallowed hard again and again, his mouth dry, his jaw juddering as if frozen to the bone. He looked down at the big book open in front of him. He could feel all the eyes of the room turned against him, waiting, impatient to see if Joseph Bradshaw could really read, could really pull this off. They all wanted him to fail, he knew that. Each person in this room would love to see him falter. Every one of them wanted him to hang. But Joseph had learned the psalm. Anne had helped him and he knew it by his heart. He knew it as he knew the fold of his fields, the turn of the weather, and the will of Bess. He knew psalm 51. So there would be no joy in any of these faces today.

Joseph took a deep breath. The room smelled heavily of damp in dark wood and sweat on the bodies of the large men, clammy now under their clothes from their walk to this room. He could sense them blinking, and in the still quiet he could hear their difficult breathing and their impatience flickering in their fingertips as they began to fidget.

Joseph took another breath and looked down at the bible. The page was yellowed and smelled like the wooden table and the seats and the clothes of the stout, sweaty men. On the page, the written word was as senseless to Joseph as the ways of women.

"Have mercy on me, oh God," he began, "according to Your steadfast love."

He stopped. There was a murmur moving in the air, gaining life as it passed from one man to another. Joseph looked up from the book laid out in front of him and glanced at the men, seated, turning to one another and then peering at Joseph from the corners of their faces.

"Mr Bradshaw," Inkerswell said. Joseph looked up at Inkerswell. The man showed no hint of emotion or even any opinion. He yelled quiet at the hurried murmurs trickling fast from the mouths of the other men present, then he fixed his dull stare on Joseph again.

"Mr Bradshaw, can you please read the passage in front of you?"

Joseph could feel his mouth become slack and his eyes ache. "I… er..." he mumbled, "I were readin' it."

An uncontrolled shower of laugher spluttered from some of the men.

"Quiet!" Inkerswell yelled again. "Mr Bradshaw," Inkerswell said again. A sigh in his heavy flesh, a shuffle in his seat. "You were not reading what is in front of you. You were reciting psalm 51, were you not?"

Joseph nodded, the confusion evident on his face.

"The passage in front of you is not psalm 51, Mr Bradshaw. I have chosen an alternative passage for you today. Can you read it?"

The room seemed smaller for a moment then, the air thinner and the eyes on him more intent, and so fierce he thought they might burn him. He glanced at the bible. The words blurred. He looked up again at Inkerswell's calm and steady expression.

"Can you read it, Mr Bradshaw?"

Joseph shook his head slightly. "No," he murmured.

"Can you speak up, Mr Bradsahaw? I don't think we all heard that."

"No," Joseph repeated. "I cannot read it."

"Because you cannot, in fact, read?" Inkerswell pressed.

Joseph felt as if his mouth would hardly move now, as if speech was stuck somewhere dried out and old in his throat.

"No," he answered. "I cannot."

Today

Glenn got out of the car and walked over to Lorraine.

"All good?" he asked.

. Lorraine was standing staring over the field, down to where the stream lurched. "Yeah," she answered, "but maybe we should go somewhere else, or maybe we shouldn't be doing this at all. I mean, I haven't even brought my toothbrush or anything."

Glenn slapped her arse while he glanced around to check no one was looking. "It's an adventure, babe," he said.

He was a total dog. One minute he was lying to his wife right in front of her, then getting all worried about Lorraine's husband finding out about the two of them, and five minutes later he was on heat again.

"Come on," he said, and he took her hand and walked her into the hotel.

It was a different room this time and for a minute Lorraine felt relief and a sense of being safe, away from the one they were in last time with the mirror and the window at the front where cars' headlights swooped over the walls. She looked around this smaller room and thought maybe it would be OK. Maybe she and Glenn would pass a normal night and tomorrow she could leave without the feeling of being chased by a slip in time.

Glenn walked towards her in the room, chest puffed, head held high, and he put his arms around her middle and pulled her to him.

"I've been waiting all day to do this," he said.

Lorraine stiffened. For maybe the first time ever his charm was having no effect. She frowned to herself. Odd. Very odd. He was a shit, and she knew that, but usually it only took a few words, a look, a touch, a kiss, and she overlooked everything else. It occurred to her then, that it wasn't enough anymore. The thought touched her lightly that she didn't want him to lie and treat her like she was just a body and nothing more. She wanted the Glenn from the last night they'd spent here. She wanted the Glenn who'd stroked her hair and cradled her in his arms and made her feel safe and cared for. She wanted the whole thing, not just sex and snatched arguments and fast passion and money and champagne and excitement. She wanted all of it. And if she couldn't have that...

He leaned down to her and began kissing her. She closed her eyes and waited to feel it consume her. But it didn't. She opened her eyes again and wriggled out of his arms.

"What's wrong now?" he asked.

Lorraine could feel his impatience flashing in his body, most of it in his trousers, she thought.

"I... I just don't feel like it, Glenn," she said. There was no doubt this was unexpected, unusual, unheard of when it came to her and Glenn, but it would certainly make things easier, there was no doubt about that.

"Don't feel like it?" he said. "But you always feel like it."

"I don't always feel like it, Glenn," she snapped.

He shrugged. "Well, OK, then, so why don't you feel like it now? It's not because of that whole ghost thing, is it? Tell me it's not that."

"It's not that."

"Well, what is it, then?"

Lorraine walked over to the only chair in the room and sat down. "If you must know, it was you talking to Julia on the phone earlier."

Glenn stood there staring at her. "What?" he said.

"When I heard you lying to her like that I felt sorry for her."

"What are you talking about? You lie to your husband all the time. And you don't even know Julia, why would you feel sorry for her?"

"Well, that's it I suppose," she said. "I don't know her. It made me think, that's all, she's your wife and you're lying to her because of me."

Glenn held his arms out away from his sides and then let them fall in an act of frustration. "So?" he said. "Why does it suddenly matter?"

"It just does," she answered. She crossed her legs in the chair, sat back and looked him over. She was going to say it now, and she watched him closely so she would be able to see every word running in his body when she spoke them. "I feel like it's wrong," she said. "It isn't fair on Julia. And I think she deserves to know."

For a minute he looked like he hadn't heard her. He seemed to make no reaction at all. Then he jolted his head forward at her in an over-emphasised look of astonishment.

"Deserves to know?" he said. "What's that supposed to mean?"

"Don't you feel bad lying to her?" she asked.

"No," he said. "Just like you don't feel bad about the lying you do."

"But this isn't about me, is it? This is about you. And Julia."

Glenn narrowed his eyes at her. "What are you playing at?" he asked.

"Who says I'm playing?"

*

They'd stared at each other like that for a few silent moments before Lorraine suddenly got up and said, "Come on, let's go down and get something to eat, I'm starving."

He watched her carefully as she moved, as if she might burn him if he got too close. He wished he could see inside her mind and understand what she was thinking. All that stuff she just said. All that about Julia. If he didn't know better he'd say she was cracking up. But Lorraine wasn't the type to fall apart. She wasn't the kind to get all sentimental. So what was she doing?

They ate in the bar of the hotel, at one of only five tables. A real fire cracked and swayed in the middle of the wall to their right and couples touched and talked over the other tables. The room was no bigger than any front room in any typical semi, and the bar was curved and the size of Lorraine's kitchen at home. Lorraine looked around and thought about her home. Small, dull, in need of work and repairs. Then she looked over at Glenn with his expensive watch and his flash car parked outside, and his wife sitting at home drinking in his lies and enjoying all that their money brought her.

Glenn ordered more champagne and the barman brought it over in an ice bucket. Lorraine could feel the other diners glancing at the decadence, but she didn't care. She deserved this.

They wouldn't mention any of that business from earlier now, she knew that. As she drank the champagne she knew the things she had said would bake. She and Glenn would drink now and then go back up to the room and do what Glenn had brought her here to do. That's all he really wanted. That's all he ever wanted her for. And she would feel her veins grow numb and her mind easy. And she'd do all the things he wanted. And she didn't mind. She didn't care. She liked it. But later, when they slept, or maybe tomorrow morning when the cold light crept into the room and the alcohol and desire was washed away, then he would find her words tumbling in his brain.

*

Glenn was quiet when he woke up the next morning. Lorraine had left the curtains with a gap between them so that the white morning light drifted in like first snow. Usually when she was with Glenn he woke up in an altogether different state. Usually he was ready for it in a morning. She would either feel him nudging her from behind or he would take her sleep-heavy hand and lay it on his body until she felt the purpose. Not today though. This morning he sat up awkwardly in the bed and passed a hand over his face before staring at the light etching itself onto the wall. He looked down at Lorraine as if she was his long-suffering wife, she opened her eyes, then he got up out of bed and stumbled to the bathroom.

Lorraine could hear him cough and bring up the toilet seat with a clatter and then turn on the shower. She could almost feel the worry and the confusion clinging to his skin.

*

"Shall we just get off?" he said, as he began to button up his shirt and pull on his trousers.

"No, wait," she answered. "Let's go for a walk."

"Not another bloody walk," he muttered.

She smiled. She had him. He was pissed off and it could only be the things she'd said yesterday that did that.

"Just down to the stream," she went on. "Looks alright, and the woman, manager or owner or whatever she is, was showing it to me yesterday while you fetched the car."

He looked up at her while he pulled on his shoes. "Since when were you into stuff like this?"

She shrugged. "Since always," she said. "You just don't know me very well, Glenn, you might think you do, but you don't."

He let go a muffled humph and did his shoe laces up.

*

Outside the sky was like a slow river. It was hard to tell where clouds ended and sky made its way through in watery dimness. The white-grey showed stretches of blue aching beneath it, but it never gave way and moved like the stream.

Lorraine walked ahead. She turned to him once and said, "Suppose I'm not really wearing the right shoes for this." To which he lifted an eyebrow and didn't answer. When would Lorraine ever wear the right shoes for this? Did she even own shoes for this?

He followed her down to the water, hands tight in his pockets. Halfway down the field he thought to himself, what am I doing? And couldn't come up with an answer. Ahead of him, he saw Lorraine's dark hair, half of it not even real, lift in the cold breeze. He took a moment to notice her shiver as her hair was blown away from her neck, and then his eyes moved down and rested where her hips swayed as she walked.

They reached the stream and Lorraine stopped and turned to face Glenn. "See," she said. "It's nice, yeah?"

"Well, yeah," he answered. "But why are we here?"

"To appreciate a nice scene."

He looked around him, unimpressed.

"That's the trouble with you," she went on. "I bet it's nice where you live. I bet whenever you want to see something nice you just have to walk outside. I bet you've got something like this all around you all the time." She swept her arm around her and then let it fall.

"What are you getting at?" he asked.

"You're not fussed about this 'cause it's normal to you, but it's not to me."

"So?"

"So, I want that. I want it to be normal to me."

"Eh? You're not making any sense, Lorraine. You want to live somewhere like this? Is that what you're going on about?"

She took a step towards him. "No," she said. "That's not what I'm going on about."

She was close to him now and he had to look down, into her face. "Well, what, then?"

"I want nice things, Glenn. I want more. I don't want to live somewhere like this. I want to live somewhere like where you live." She turned away quickly and took a couple of steps towards the stream. Then she looked all around her as if she was breathing the sky and the water and the uninterrupted field into her body. "And like I said yesterday, I feel sorry for Julia, I think she kinda deserves to know what's going on."

Glenn stared at her. "Whatever you think you're playing at, it's a dangerous game."

She matched his stare and stood perfectly still. "I'm not playing, Glenn," she said.

He was looking right at her. The air that surrounded her, the trees, the stream, the grass and the horizon, were all a blur around her. She was the focus. She was all he was looking at. Her words a puzzle inside his body now, passed from her to him, and he couldn't figure it. He was staring at her, but slowly like the slide of mud down a hill, he began to notice something else. They weren't alone. There was someone else there with them. Glenn's first thought was that someone had heard everything they'd been saying. Either someone was deliberately there with them or they'd just happened on them. But the thought of this private, awkward conversation being heard was enough to rip his eyes away from the waiting Lorraine.

He looked sharply to the right. He'd been aware of a figure standing there, just where the trees overhung the stream down behind Lorraine. He knew Lorraine was still staring at him, but he was drawn away from her face and into the face of a girl standing by the stream, no, in the stream, no, that was stupid, beside the stream. He peered at the girl. She was dressed funny, old-fashioned, and it looked as if her hair was wet, hanging lank and dirty by her face and over her shoulders. She stood with her arms straight by her sides and her knees together. As Glenn's eyes focussed on the girl he could see there was something wrong with her face. She was very pale, not just fair-skinned but really pale, like she'd never been outdoors or something. Her eyes were very round and watery and she looked... cold, but the thing that really made him bolt was the skin on her cheeks. Her skin under her eyes and covering her cheekbones and above her brows appeared broken. He stared harder for a moment, until he was sure her skin was damaged in some way. He was about to move towards her and check she was OK when he saw the broken skin on her face begin to ooze. He swallowed hard and grabbed Lorraine's arm in front of him. There was liquid, water he was sure, dribbling down the girl's face now.

"Oh, God," he said. He was vaguely aware of Lorraine moving in front of him, saying "What's a matter?"

Glenn lifted his arm to point at the girl, her eyes bulging and water streaming from the skin on her face now. Lorraine turned around and then back to Glenn, saying, "What? What's wrong with you?" But Glenn was moving, stumbling backwards up the field, and then turning and running all the way up to the car.

*

Lorraine reached the car door and tried to open it. Glenn was sitting there fiddling with the ignition. She banged on the

130

door. "Glenn!"

He turned and looked at her. Lorraine had never seen him look like this before. He was visibly shaking, his face the colour of cooled ash. He reached out and unlocked the passenger door from the inside and Lorraine slipped into the seat.

"What's wrong with you?" she asked.

He stared at her. "That girl," he said.

"What girl?"

"The one down there just then."

He was shouting now and Lorraine tried to calm him. "Slow down," she said. "What girl? I didn't see any girl."

"You must have. She was standing down there by the stream, in it, I don't know, but she was standing there and her face was..."

She stared at him and waited for the words, her impatience edging from her. "Her face was what?"

He was quieter now, as if speaking it lifted the panic. "I don't know," he said. "It was like, scarred or something, but not scars, wounds, and there was something coming out of the wounds, liquid, just looked like water, didn't you see her? You must have seen her."

She shook her head. "I didn't see anybody." Her mind began to double over. The stream. He just said the girl was in the stream. She thought through the story the woman from the hotel had told her and all the times she had seen and felt things round here herself. There was something very wrong with this place.

Glenn was looking straight ahead now. He shifted in his seat. "We should go back," he said. "Do you think we should go back? Maybe she needs help."

Lorraine thought for a moment. He was surely talking about the same thing, whatever it was, that she had seen herself. He hadn't believed her, and she supposed that was understandable, it did sound crazy, but now he had seen it too... hadn't he? The only thing that made her unsure was the way he described the girl's face. What was it he'd said? Sores of some sort or wounds or something. Lorraine hadn't seen anything like that when she'd seen that girl. When she'd seen her it had been a normal-looking girl, apart from the clothing of course, that she'd seen. There hadn't been anything visibly wrong with her, but Glenn seemed to be shaken by the appearance of the girl more than her actual presence. It seemed to have scared him to look at her.

She thought, what if there was a girl down there, a normal, real girl who was hurt in some way and needed help? What if it was as simple as that? If that was the case – if – then perhaps he was right.

"OK," she answered. "Let's go back and if she's there we can go and see if she's OK." Lorraine could hear her own words coming out slowly and precisely. This was crazy. She turned and got out of the car again. They both stood by their doors for a moment and Glenn looked hesitantly down the hill.

"Come on, then," Lorraine said, and she walked ahead of him, down towards the stream.

Once she got to the place they had stood in before she turned to see Glenn following her, his feet making dents in the grass as he dug his heels into the slope. Lorraine looked all around and then flapped her arms out by her sides.

"See?" she said. "No one here."

Glenn still looked nervous and he seemed to be struggling with what to say. "She was here," he answered. "She was here."

*

They walked back up the hill towards the hotel. From this angle, Lorraine could see how the picture on the wall in the hotel had been sketched. This was the perspective the artist had on the scene. Behind her now was the stream, she was standing right here where the figures in the picture were, and behind her, on top of the slope, was the building, now a hotel, once Hill Head House. The hotel faced to the left, towards the village, but according to the picture, Hill Head House had faced the opposite way, to the right, with the summit of the hill just beyond it. She stopped for a moment and thought about what it must have been like to have lived here back then, how scared the villagers must have been at that time, and how they would cling to anything, anyone they thought could help them.

Glenn was walking ahead. He hadn't said much else since they'd been back down there and looked for the girl. Lorraine moved a little faster now and caught up with him. She touched his arm and he turned quickly.

"Now do you believe me?" she asked.

Glenn shook her off. "I'm not saying I believe anything."

"But you saw her. You saw her too."

"I saw something, someone."

"Come on, Glenn, you know that wasn't... you know that was no ordinary girl you saw down there, you said yourself, her face..."

He stopped walking and looked directly in Lorraine's eyes now. "Did she look like that when you saw her?"

Lorraine struggled with her words. "I... no, she looked... like a girl, I mean there was nothing wrong with her."

"So why did I see her like that, then?" he asked. "Why did she look like that when I saw her?"

Lorraine thought for a moment. The story about what had happened here. The murder. The girl. The man; bloody men. It was like the girl was coaxing Lorraine to something, trying to lead her somewhere, but when Glenn saw her... it was grotesque, by the sounds of it, by his reaction to it.

"She was killed," Lorraine said. "Murdered. By a married man she was seeing..."

Glenn looked her intently as she spoke. "What are you saying?" he asked. "She thinks I'm him or something?"

"No, no." Lorraine shook her head, still thinking through the story and all that had happened, was happening. "I don't know – no, I shouldn't think so. I don't know, I mean I don't know, but, maybe, if what we are seeing is a ghost..." she tipped her head to the sky and laughed at her own words, but really, what was the point in not saying it now? However crazy it sounded. Then she brought her face level with Glenn's again. "Maybe there is a reason. Maybe there's a reason I see her fine and you saw her like that."

"What reason?"

"You're a man."

"So?"

"It was a man who killed her. A married man she was having an affair with."

"So, she wants..."

Lorraine shrugged. "Revenge."

Glenn turned away from her and looked up at the hotel. "This is ridiculous," he said. "I'm leaving."

"We'd better go in and get our stuff," Lorraine said. "We haven't checked out or anything."

"Yeah," Glenn muttered. "And then, that's it, I'm never coming back here."

Derbyshire, 1760s

Anne made her way to the room he was kept in only once. It was cold. She put her hand to the wall to steady herself as she entered, and felt the lumpy stone damp to the touch. Anne was experiencing a light-headedness when she moved around too quickly, as if the sun was constantly beating her brain, and she found the fear of fainting chased her each day.

Joseph was being kept here until he was hanged. Anne knew it. In the parts of her brain that knew the close responsibility of another human being would soon be upon her, and that Bess would not live out more than another three winters, she knew it. But she couldn't let herself fully inspect any of these realities. She had no experience with these things, couldn't recognise how they would fit.

Anne put one hand to the cold, damp stone of the wall and the other to the underside of her belly, still small, a hardness no one else could see where the baby formed, and she smiled at the young man standing guard at the room. She was looked on with suspicion, or pity, or anger, she couldn't tell.

"Five minutes!" was barked at her.

She went quietly inside and found Joseph sitting up, winding a piece of cloth around his own hands. He looked up as she entered and she saw a blanket of self-pity and anger laid in his skin.

He eyed the way she held her stomach, his face turned half away from her as if the swell there was a threat to him, could hurt him.

"Yer not to worry, my love," she said.

She sat down beside him as he dipped his head and he smiled sadly to himself.

"Not to worry?" he said. "Yer plan din't work. I'll 'ang."

"Yer mun't think like that," she said, laying her hand on his. She felt him still and cold beneath her fingers, not responding. She struggled for a moment with what to say, then she took his hand and laid it on her belly.

"Yer can't give up," she said. "Yer 'ave a reason to live right 'ere. Our baby, Joseph."

Joseph snatched his hand away and Anne saw it withdraw into a fist in his lap. "Are yer mad, woman?" he snapped. "Yer think that'll 'elp?" he motioned to her body with the fist and she flinched slightly. "That can't 'elp me. Nothing can 'elp me now."

"But it's our baby, Joseph."

"And what of it? Yer think a bairn changes anything? It dun't change nothing."

Anne was silent for a moment. She felt her body shrink away from him slightly. He was making her a fool, right there in that room, he was making her the idiot. She'd really believed in the bond this baby would strengthen. She hung onto it still. He didn't know what he was saying. He was afraid, no one could blame him for that. He was facing... she didn't want to think about what he might be facing, but it was understandable he would react like this... wasn't it?

"It gives yer 'ope, surely?" she said quietly.

He turned to her then and she saw his face full of anger. For perhaps the first time ever she saw something ugly in her husband. Anne's features seemed to lock and she sat still waiting for whatever was to come from him.

"'Ope?" he spat. "'Ow does this give me 'ope? I never asked for this. Yer bring this to me, now, and yer talk of 'ope?"

"But I'm your wife, Joseph, it's natural that we should 'ave a child, it's God's will."

"And is me 'anging God's will an' all?" He blew air out between his teeth and turned away from her, seemed to build more words in his chest and then turned back on her again. "Yer talk of God, yer know nothing about these things." Then he pointed his finger at her face and he looked at her as if she was nothing. "Sarah knew. She understood me. She knew the darkness, 'ow it comes on a man, 'ow it takes over. She knew."

Anne shook her head, her face filled with fear and panic now.

"What are you saying, Jospeh? What is this?"

"It were an accident," he said. "I never meant to 'urt her, but she 'ad me in such a place." He screwed up his hands tightly in his lap again. "She 'ad me so... we were like animals, do yer 'ear, animals! And I couldn't stop it. She 'ad me like a man gone mad."

Anne shifted her face away from him now, looking at him with alarm from the sides of her eyes. "What do you mean?" she asked.

"I mean, we 'ad the devil in us, Anne! Me and Sarah, we were the same like that. So don't talk to me about God, God was nowhere when I took Sarah up t' the trees of a night. God din't stop me." Then he leaned into Anne, her body instantly pulling away from him, and he took hold of her hands and her arm roughly. "I took Sarah up there like I've never taken a woman before or since, do yer 'ear me? I took 'er and not neither me nor 'er could stop it. We 'ad the devil in us alright. And I'm not sorry for that."

He dropped his hold on her and she felt her face drain and her words dry and heavy in her mouth. "Yer not sorry?"

He looked straight ahead of him now, his anger dispersed in the air between them. "No, I'm not. I'm sorry she's dead, that's all. I never wanted that. I'm sorry it was 'er I killed and not you."

*

It was months later when she left the house for good. Her mother said it should happen. She arranged it. Anne's aunt in Sheffield said she would take her, at least until her confinement was over.

Anne packed her things and left, before she became too big to manage the journey. She held onto her bag, Bess obedient now by her heels, and she closed the door behind her. She had no idea if she would ever come back to this place.

Spring had brought its freshness to the sky and the earth and the air she breathed. She felt it lift her for the briefest moment as she stood outside the house and, for that moment, she thought she could face anything.

The fields lay untended and she had no image of what

might happen to them. She had successfully sold all the livestock Joseph had kept, the money from which had seen her through so far, but that was running low. It pained her to see Joseph's work go to waste as it did, but Anne had no way of seeing an alternative.

She looked down, the bag in her hand, at Bess sitting and waiting for what would come next. Then she walked to the edge of the house and looked up to the trees. There, somewhere, Sarah lay. No one had made any effort to find her and move her as far as Anne knew. Though she knew Mr Vernon had sought out the parson and asked his advice on the fate of Sarah's soul. The parson had soothed him and had asked Anne's permission to visit the area and conduct a service. He had knocked at her door one day, sending Bess barking and Anne struggling with her countenance as she opened the door to him. She didn't ask him in, but tried to remain still while he asked her.

"It would help lay the poor girl to rest," he had said. "No one is blaming you, Anne, we all know you had no knowledge of this terrible act, but still this is something you can do to put things right on your husband's behalf... since he cannot. Let us onto your land for this. All we ask is access to the wooded area behind the house."

Anne had stood there facing the parson and she had felt a rage like she had never felt before. They wanted that girl to be at peace. That whore. They asked Anne to let them here so they could give that girl peace. Sarah Vernon. Not a chance. Sarah Vernon did not deserve peace. She deserved an eternity of sorrow for what she had done.

"I'm sorry," she had replied. "But I can't let yer onto my land. My 'usband din't do this terrible thing yer speak of and Sarah Vernon dun't lie 'ere on this land." Then she had closed the door, her hands trembling so much she struggled with the lock.

Now she stood in this cool morning and she gazed at the trees where her husband had taken Sarah, taken her, then killed her and laid her. Bess watched eagerly. No one, including the dog, had been up there since, though Anne felt

Sarah around all the time. Not when she was inside the house, not even at night; once the door was closed and she and Bess were inside it was just the two of them. And the baby. But outside, around the stone of the house, in the field, by the bushes, even in the lane, Anne felt Sarah near to her all the time. She couldn't explain it, and she didn't tell anyone, but if she had, she would have said she simply felt her. Like the clinging mist. Like a whiff of smoke. Like fine drizzle you can't see but that soaks you to the skin.

Anne walked slowly around the house she was leaving now. She took her steps carefully, as if each one was full of importance. She came to the place where the grass gave way to earth and fallen leaves and she walked up the steady incline until she was amongst the trees. Here she stopped for a moment. The baby was heavy inside her and its movements were becoming duller now there was less room for its limbs. She supported her belly with her cupped hand underneath it for a minute or two, then she took a deep breath and walked a little further. Once she was amongst the trees she stopped again. Bess stood and waited, but when nothing else happened the dog stood back and began to bark. Anne looked around her. She had no way of knowing where Sarah was. She could be standing above her right now and she wouldn't know. She looked at Bess. "Where is she?" she said. "Come on girl, where is she?" The dog whimpered a little and still looked expectantly at Anne. "Where is she?" Anne asked again. She held out her arms by her sides then let them fall in frustration. This was hopeless. She had no thought of why she had come up here like this. She should just leave. She was angry and hurt still and her emotions rushed inside her till she thought she would break. The full enormity of all that had happened seemed to only just become clear. She thought she would sit down on the damp earth right now and never get up again. The happiness in her life was gone. Her hope was gone.

But she didn't sit down. She stood and watched, as if in a dream, as Bess began to rake at the soft ground with her claws. The dog was quiet now, focussed on what she was doing. Anne observed her for a moment. Her feet worked fast, earth flicking in the air behind her, then she pushed her nose into the cool ground. "Is that it, Bess?" Anne asked. "Is that where she is?"

Bess stopped and looked up at Anne, barking again. Anne smiled, and as quickly as the smile had come, it was followed by a feeling of confusion. What had she expected to do once she was here? She looked down on the area of earth Bess had been digging. And she felt the open air and the sky and the fields all around her. And herself, tiny and insignificant. Her world ripped apart by this she-devil. The anger tightened inside her again and she bent down and spat into the clawed earth.

"Damn your soul to hell, Sarah Vernon," she said. "May you never find peace!"

*

Anne took a last, long look at the house as she stood near the lane. Her throat felt tight and narrow and a rush of emotion spread inside her. Her brain did its best to hold onto what had happened here, but the events stretched like the open fields all around and Anne felt she would never leave it behind her. She felt she would walk this area forever, no matter how much distance she put between herself and all that had happened. Her being would always be trapped in this time and this place. Like Sarah, she thought, the earth holding onto her, never letting go.

She stepped into the lane and she looked down and saw Bess's eyes sad, her head dipped by Anne's legs and her tail low.

"Me and you, Bess," she said. "It's just me and you now. And this baby – that's all we 'ave now."

As she looked up again she saw the familiar figure of a man ahead in the lane. He was running his palms against the bush by the road, watching as the new green leaves prickled and feathered his skin. In his other hand he held a bag filled with all he had collected so far that day. The sight of Aaron kicked a memory into the front of Anne's mind. It had been months ago now, before the swell in her belly could be seen, before anyone else in the village knew about it. Anne had walked Bess into the lane. She didn't go far on account of the nausea which kept on taking over her body. She'd felt that the cool, sharp air would help and maybe liven her, she was so tired all the time, but as she stood in the lane with Bess she felt the retch begin and the saliva quicken in her mouth.

Anne had vomited twice in the lane when she looked up, wiping her mouth with her sleeve, and saw Aaron approaching her. Anne's first instinct was to turn and leave fast, no one here had a kind word for Anne anymore, and she couldn't face it while she felt so weak. But as she watched the man coming closer to her Anne had a strange feeling of calm.

"Let me help you," he said, as he came up near to her.

Anne pushed her hand over her face and watched Aaron suspiciously. "No need," she said.

"There is every need," Aaron went on. "I must see you into your home."

"No, really, I am quite alright."

"You are not alright, Anne."

She looked up at him then. The familiar use of her name startled her. He said it as if they were friends when they barely knew each other.

"Here, let me help you." He took her hand and laid her arm in his, then he began walking her back towards the house. "Though, you must understand this is nothing to be alarmed about," he said as they walked. "Sickness such as this can only mean the baby is healthy and its attachment strong."

She looked at him sharply. "'Ow did yer know?"

"I see it in your eyes, Anne," he answered. "Soon everyone will be able to see it in your body."

Once they got back to the house Aaron sat Anne at the kitchen table. "I have to go for a few moments, and I'll bring back with me something to help with the sickness."

Anne nodded dumbly at him. It was true, the things that were said about him, he did know things. Just like his mother had. Even Bess was calm and seemed to look up to him.

When he returned, Aaron brought with him a strange-looking object Anne had never seen before. He stayed for hours in Anne's house and boiled the object, then presented Anne with the liquid to drink.

"What is it?" she asked.

"Ginger," he replied. "This will keep the feeling of the sickness away, only for a short time, you understand, the sickness is your body's way and it can't be stopped altogether or perhaps the baby would be stopped also, but it will help you to go about your business."

Anne sipped the hot liquid while he talked.

"You must rest as much as possible, eat lots of bread and let sleep take you whenever it will."

She nodded her head as he left her, promising to return with more ginger so Anne could prepare the drink for herself.

When he returned, Anne asked how she could compensate him.

"No," he answered, and he waved his hand in front of him to dismiss the idea. "It is the least I can do."

As she watched him for a moment now, standing in the lane, Bess looking expectantly ahead, she wondered what he had meant by that. But he was a good man, she didn't doubt at all, and she was sure whatever he meant, it was pure.

*

Anne and Bess turned the other way, away from the lane that led down to the village, away from Aaron, and up, up, to the peak of the hill, up to the rise of the land and the swell of the sky. They walked until Anne could see the other side. Her feet forced the stones aside on the dirt track and Bess wandered around rocks and boulders, stretching her legs to urinate and then trotting ahead. Anne felt the case drag in her hand, the sword she carried with her like a whispered reminder of what she should remember, and she shifted her weight, her back struggling with the extra load. Her body had grown steadily used to the child growing and shifting in her, but her possessions in the case felt cumbersome. The baby was as heavy as Anne's sadness, as unknown as her future and as frightening as her past. Over the last few weeks and months, Anne had looked around her and felt as if she was truly adrift.

142

Her recent past chased her every move but the future was a hazy shadow she couldn't plainly see.

"It will be well," her mother had said. "In Sheffield. Yer aunt will see yer right, and I reckon it's better to leave that 'ouse, that place, now. Yer've nothing but bad memories, girl, and yer need some light now."

As Anne and Bess made their way over the tops, Anne hoped her mother was right. She held a hand under her belly and breathed in the thin air. She had to look forward now, she knew this, for the baby.

*

Hill Head House stood quiet. A large tombstone to a small grave behind it. An empty vessel. A poisoned home no one would ever want to live in again. Bess's scratch marks at the door. The cold grate where a fire was once lit.

With Anne gone, no one went up to the house at all anymore. It stood dark and cold at night, the sky seeming to pass over it swiftly, the wind seeming to move around it without touching it, not wanting to get too close. Like everybody. Like all the people in the village. No one went up there. But someone came down from there.

*

Nobody is sure of the first time it happened. The landlord's wife said she saw it first as she stepped outside for a breath of fresh air one stuffy, busy night. The Kingston Arms was full that evening and one or two of the men had begun to argue. She didn't know what over, but once they had enough beer inside them they were likely to argue over the smallest things. Her husband always did his best to stay out of the disagreements of the other men, and had, in her opinion, the patience of a saint. She lacked the same, and tonight she stepped out of the door and took a long, cool breath to calm her annoyance. She stood with her back to the wall. On one side of her was the steps down into the inn, the "low drop", on the other side of her was the low window, the men's reddened faces and inflated angers just beyond it. She took another deep breath and closed her eyes for a moment, leaning her head back against the stone. They were arguing about stupid things again in there. Things that couldn't be changed. Things that had been and gone now and no one could do a thing about. But they held onto that bad business like a dog. Some of them, she thought, would never let it go.

It was when she opened her eyes again that she saw it. It was just a flash, and she stood upright quickly and caught her breath in her throat. It was a person. It was quick, and as she took a step forward from the wall and looked around in the road she doubted herself for a second. But she had seen it. She'd seen a human form dart quick in front of her. And not just anyone, she would tell her husband and, shaking a little, the whole of the inn. It wasn't just any old person she'd seen run past her. She'd stake her life on it. She'd swear on the bible. It was Sarah. It was the ghost of Sarah Vernon.

*

The landlord's wife would claim she was the first to see it, but Inkerswell's cook would lay claim to that as well.

She saw it one night as she scrubbed the pans after dinner downstairs. She was intent on the pan and the scrubbing motion her hand made, the force she needed to bear down to get the pan clean. She looked up for just a second. The darkness outside was like a stretch of water beneath the sky, she couldn't tell where the glass of the window pane ended and the blackness of the night began. But she saw it. She dropped the pan and felt her breath wheeze in her chest. The face she saw in the window was fluid and distorted, but it was a face. She instantly put her hand to her bosom and then looked sharply behind her, not knowing what she expected. A figure perhaps, causing a reflection in the glass. A ghost right there in the room with her. But there was no one behind her, and she turned quickly back to the window. There was no one in front of her now, either. The face was gone. But it had been there. She'd lay her life on it. She'd seen the face of Sarah Vernon.

*

When she told this in the village, the constable's young sweetheart said she too had a similar experience. She blushed and became quite agitated as she told of how she had felt a presence on a couple of occasions now, how the soft breeze had played around her neck causing her to shiver, and she was sure she heard a whisper at night that could only be the ghost of Sarah Vernon. She also told the cook that she'd heard from her sweetheart about the landlord's wife and how she was scared to go out at night now.

"It's 'er alright," the cook said. "''Ow can the poor girl rest after what 'appened to 'er? It's 'er."

"Should we be afraid?" someone asked.

"She's not of this world now, none of us knows what she can do."

*

After a couple of weeks no one really knew how it had started or who had seen it first. The ghost of Sarah Vernon had been seen or felt or heard by almost everyone. And those who hadn't yet experienced it lived in fear that they would. The women hurried in doors when the blue of the sky deepened to ink, and the men stopped walking in the lane and down to the Kingston Arms once the sun had gone down. The whole village was living in a state of terror.

*

The landlord of the Kingston Arms walked up out of the village on this morning. He walked the lane as it bent around and up towards Hill Head House. But he didn't go to Hill Head House. He came to the curve in the road and the bushes and he dipped down on the grass, down towards the stream. He could see the water tumbling over rocks and fallen twigs as he approached the place where the trees shied into the hills and the little Mattson hovel stood.

He walked down on the grass to the door of the hovel and he knocked gently. When the door was answered he seemed almost shocked that it had been, and for a moment couldn't speak. Part of him had thought he could avoid this meeting altogether, but something had to be done, no matter what he thought or believed, this had to happen.

Aaron stood and looked at him, but didn't say anything.

"I... I wish to speak with yer," the landlord said.

Aaron stood aside and motioned for the landlord to enter the hovel. Once inside, the landlord looked around the small dwelling. Everywhere he looked there seemed to be an object. Things he had never seen before. Plants, dry, were hanging in bundles, tied by string, on the wall and some from the ceiling. As he turned to his right he caught sight of a small animal of some kind hanging by its feet, dead and rigid. The place smelled strongly of old smoke and herbs and body odour and other things the landlord couldn't place. He turned quickly to meet Aaron's eyes.

"I'm not sayin' I believe it," he said. "But others do, and... enough of 'em do now, for it be causing... trouble."

Aaron still didn't say anything but peered directly into the landlord's eyes and fingered his beard slightly.

"I'm talking about that girl, the one who were killed. Everyone's sayin' she's... 'aunting the place. Yer must've 'eard."

Aaron nodded.

"Then... you can do somert, 'elp in some way. People are too afraid to leave their 'omes at night, they say she's 'aunting the land, and... and the men have stopped comin' down to t' Low Drop."

"What would you have me do?"

"Get rid of it, 'er, whatever it is yer do."

"You said you don't believe it."

"I..." The landlord took a step closer to Aaron and dropped his voice as if anyone could hear him. "I don't say I don't or I do. Somert's going on, my own wife is scared, she reckons to've seen it 'erself." Then he stood back again and glanced around him. "There's no one else can 'elp us."

Aaron seemed to think for a moment before he spoke again. "And what does your wife say about the girl? Does she know why this is happening?"

"She has a notion... that the girl is searching."

"Searching? For what?"

"For 'im who killed 'er. She thinks that's why the girl is still 'ere, going round the place, looking."

"I see. You think she wants revenge? Is that what your wife thinks?"

The landlord was staring wide-eyed at Aaron now, the enormity of the situation becoming ever more real to him. "Yes!" he said. "That's it."

"No, I don't think it is," Aaron replied. He could see the landlord's face collect a frown and him narrow his eyes slightly. "Your wife is right about Sarah looking for Joseph," Aaron went on. "But she doesn't seek revenge. Sarah Vernon loved Joseph Bradshaw, I have seen it, she doesn't understand how or why she died, all she knows is she has the desire to get to him and it won't leave her. She looks for him because her heart tells her to. And she won't stop."

*

"Will you 'elp us?"

Aaron moved to the door and opened it for the landlord to leave. He stood back and didn't meet the landlord's eyes now. The landlord hesitated in the doorway. "Will you 'elp us?" he repeated.

Aaron had seen Anne leave the house earlier that day. He'd watched her from the lane as she struggled with her bag and the weight of the baby not yet born, Bess trotting obediently by her ankles. It was clear to Aaron that she was going somewhere else to have that baby. He wasn't surprised. She'd hardly want to have the baby round here, where no one spoke to her and only muttered when she passed. She would most likely go to her family, he thought. And that was for the best. If she came back at all, Aaron thought, it wouldn't be for a while.

Aaron still didn't look the landlord in the eyes, but seemed lost in thought till he spoke again. "I will need compensating."

"Compensating?"

"Yes. You wish me to do you all this... service. I can

help you with this, but my means are small here." And he held out his palm and moved it slightly as if running it in water.

"Aye," the landlord said, "I see." Then he nodded. "Aye, I can't speak for t' rest of 'em, but I know some as will be 'appy to give money. We'll compensate yer. So, yer'll do it?"

Aaron looked at him now and smiled. "I will come tomorrow," he said. "Just as the sun leaves and the darkness begins."

The landlord nodded silently and left the little house. Aaron shut the door once he had gone and leaned back against the wall. He breathed in deeply as if to calm himself, though he felt as if he had control at that moment. He closed his eyes and lifted his head to face the ceiling. "Oh, Mother," he whispered. "This is a bad business." Then he opened his eyes and moved away from the wall. He needed a plan now. He needed to work out exactly what he would have to do tomorrow evening to stop this madness. He would sit and think and, as always, the right path would reveal itself to him. He moved over to where the cold ashes of the fire lay like meaningless dreams from the night before, and he sat down. He breathed slowly again, calmly emptying his mind. In deeply, his breath cold in his nose and lungs, and out heavily with the words "It's not over", his lips moving only slightly as he thought the words then let them slip from him with the air from his body – not over yet.

Joseph was gone, and he'd thought that would be the end of it. Thought he could sleep easy again, and his conscience was clear. He'd done the right thing, done the right thing in the end. He was sure of it. He should be absolved. But it seemed these people here would not let it go.

Aaron sat on the dusty ground and he tried to calm himself. Maybe it was because they didn't know Joseph's final destination, as Aaron did. Maybe because they had not been there right at the end and seen him for themselves. As he had. But that was something Aaron had sworn to keep to himself. Inkerswell was right about that, these people would not swallow that easily.

So this one last thing had to be done. And then they could all be free of Joseph Bradshaw and Sarah Vernon.

*

The next evening, when the sun had seemed low all day and the people had needed to shield their eyes as they went about, the moon at last took its place in the sky and the villagers gathered in the street. They hadn't done anything like this for days and weeks now. They hadn't dared to venture outside once a hint of darkness came to the sky. Everyone had grown so used to staying indoors, once it was dark, they felt as if they were sneaking now while they huddled together and made a show of saying it was cold. It wasn't that cold, not compared to the weeks and months just gone, but, all the same, Inkerswell's cook held her own body tightly and George stamped his feet on the tough ground.

"What's tha reckon 'e'll do?" one of the men asked.

George looked up. "'E'll see to it," he answered

They fell silent again. The constable stood with his arm round his girl, her small jaw juddering with the cold or nerves or sheer fright. The landlord and his wife, dulled and eased by ale from the Kingston Arms, stood together at the edge of the group of people, saying nothing, the landlord looking to the hill all the time for the figure they all waited for. When he saw him, the landlord felt the relief flood his body like no ale could.

"'E's 'ere!" he said, and he lifted his arm to point to the shadowy vision of Aaron coming down the hill.

There was a shiver of whispers and muttering as they each looked to see Aaron walking fast over the land. When he approached the group of waiting villagers it was as if he had a power none of them had been aware of before, including himself. He felt it swell and make him taller.

"I will need a silver bowl," he said.

They all looked at each other. Inkerswell lifted his head in acknowledgment. "I'll have one." Then he looked to his cook who stood nearby, and together they walked away in the direction of Inkerswell's house.

While they waited, Aaron stood apart from the other

villagers with his back turned. When Inkerswell and his cook came back with the bowl, Aaron turned to face them, his head slightly bowed, his hand around his beard. Then he looked up, straight into the eyes of the magistrate. If it hadn't been so dark someone might have noticed the look which passed between Inkerswell and Aaron then. But it was slight, just a quiet shared secret, and the thin shine in their eyes as they snatched each other's vision for just a second, wasn't seen by anyone. He took the bowl as it was held out to him and without looking at any of them he said, "Follow me."

*

They walked in the lowering darkness, the wind becoming stronger the higher they went. They walked up and out of the village and back the way Aaron had come.

"Where is 'e taking us?" the landlord's wife whispered.

"'Appen we're goin' to 'is 'ouse," her husband said.

She looked at him doubtfully, the shadows on his face showing how tired he was. They all were. The sooner this business was over, she thought, the better. Then they could all go back to normal and the men would be back in the Low Drop, laughing and drinking and fighting now and then, the ghost of this poor girl in their past.

They walked on to the bend and the dip in the road, where the bushes shielded the land, and on past the place where the hovel hugged the hills. They walked a few more minutes before their destination was in sight. When it was, another shiver ran through the group of villagers. But not with whispered words this time, not full of their muttering and speculation, only a shiver of apprehension and fear. They all seemed to slow and some stop completely as they realised where Aaron was taking them. They rounded the hill and along the lane and there stood the dark, cold form of Hill Head House.

*

Aaron walked swiftly around the bushes and towards the house. He glanced behind him to make sure they were all

150

following, and noticed one or two holding back. He peered over his shoulder in the darkness to try and make out who was reluctant. George and Mr Vernon. They were muttering to each other, their hands deep in their pockets, their shoulders hunched in to one another. It was understandable, Aaron thought, it was hardly a surprise.

He ushered the bulk of the villagers around by the side of the house and then moved his way to the back of the group. George and Mr Vernon looked up at him as he approached them.

"Now then, lad," George said. "What's tha thinking 'ere?"

"Sarah..."

Mr Vernon took a step forward. "You don't touch my Sarah!" he shouted.

The villagers huddled together in the cold and found a silence settle on them as they watched the three men.

Aaron put a hand on Mr Vernon's arm and tried to calm him. "I will not harm your daughter," he said. "You have my word. I merely wish to see her at peace."

Mr Vernon stared at him in the darkness. "But yer not goin' to..." He motioned towards the trees in a jerky movement with his hand. "Not in front of all these people, not like this, not for this purpose."

Aaron closed his eyes and shook his head very slightly. "No," he answered. "Her body won't be disturbed. It is not me who has ever sought to do that, remember?"

Mr Vernon appeared stung by the words, tangled with the memory of the night he had been ready to dig his daughter up along with Sandy and Inkerswell. Then he felt the shame of that night and what he'd been prepared to do, and he dipped his head and nodded at Aaron.

"It's not her body we have to deal with," Aaron said. "Now please wait here." Aaron turned to the other villagers. "If you would all just wait here, there is something I have to collect. Mr Inkerswell... the bowl I asked for." He held out his hand and Inkerswell handed him a silver bowl. With that, Aaron turned and walked back the way they had just come.

Some people stood on tiptoes to follow his form as he walked back down towards the lane, some huddled together and speculated about what would happen now, some stood silently, already anxious about the night. Only the constable walked slowly after him. He walked into the darkness, the flitting figure of Aaron in his sights. He watched as Aaron walked quickly down to the stream, the silver bowl in his loose hand by his side. Then he watched as Aaron bent at the stream, then turned to walk back, the bowl held in front of him. The constable rushed back up to the others, afraid he'd been seen.

"What's 'e doing?" someone asked.

"'E bent down at t' stream. I din't see 'im proper, but it looked like he was fetching water from t' stream."

The people looked at each other, some in wonder, some in confusion.

"'Appen it's that, then," the cook said. "And t' water's for' er." She pointed behind her at the trees where they all knew Sarah lay.

"What'll 'e do with stream water?" the landlord's wife asked.

"I don't know, do I?" the cook answered. "Pour it on 'er, I should imagine. 'E'll 'appen make it right first, the water, so as it does what 'e wants, so it can 'elp, 'er to move over."

They fell silent again as they waited for Aaron to return, some thinking about what the cook had just said, some imagining what Aaron would do, some doubting it.

When they saw him walking carefully back towards them, the bowl held in front of him, they stiffened, and anxiety ran among them again. As he approached them and they pushed each other a little to each get a look at the bowl, they took their breaths in a short and bewildered manner. In the darkness, they could see the shine of the moon on the silver of the bowl and the reflection in the water shimmying like a wobble in glass. And there in the water, flapping and beating itself against the bowl, lay a fish.

*

152

Mr Vernon stood back in alarm when he saw the fish.

"What's tha doing with that?" he asked.

"Be still," Aaron answered. Then he turned to face Mr Vernon. "Sir, you must understand, your daughter is stuck in this place. She roams the land here because she does not wish to move on."

Mr Vernon stared at him in the darkness.

"It's no fault of hers, but she is causing distress to everyone here."

"What are yer saying?"

"I am saying she has to move on."

"And what will t' fish do?"

"The fish will not do anything... but accept Sarah."

Mr Vernon shook his head quickly. "I don't understand."

Aaron was moving towards the trees at the back of the house and the villagers followed. "I must do this now and return the fish to the stream. Some space, please."

"Do what?" Mr Vernon shouted. "What is it yer doin'?"

Aaron still held the bowl in front of him as he moved up into the trees. He seemed to know exactly where to go and the villagers all stayed back out of fear and anxiety over what would happen now.

"I said, what are yer doin'?" Mr Vernon shouted again. "That's my daughter, I've a right to know!"

The constable grabbed hold of Mr Vernon as he tried to go into the trees after Aaron. Aaron stopped for just a second, the bowl held out in front of him, and turned his head slightly, the darkness making him a shadow, the trees ready to swallow him and the moon moving overhead between the branches like snatches of sky beneath clouds.

"I am going to relieve this village of its ghost, sir," Aaron answered. "And in the process I will set your daughter free. From now on, she will only haunt the stream."

There was a gasp from the group of villagers as Mr Vernon stood in the constable's clutches, his body frozen by what he was witnessing. And Aaron moved into the trees until he had disappeared, his voice trailing behind him.

*

When he reappeared he moved swiftly past the people and back down towards the stream, calling after him as he went, "The spirit of Sarah Vernon now dwells in this fish, which I shall release back into the stream."

The people watched him go, some in awe, some in doubt. And Mr Vernon sat on the ground by the trees with his head in his hands, George by his side.

A Bad Winter

Today

They walked back into the hotel. Lorraine first, Glenn behind her. Up the wide staircase with its glossed, dark wood and its deep, red carpet, and to their room on the first floor. Once inside, Lorraine flopped her body down onto the bed, pretty floral quilt and satin throw beneath her. She lay with her arms flung out by her sides and her legs crossed slightly as if she was totally relaxed.

Glenn stood and frowned. "What are you doing?" he asked. "Come on, let's get going."

Lorraine let her feet fall and dangled them over the edge of the bed, swaying them like a child on a swing. "Suppose..." she said. "Suppose our ghost is trying to tell me something." She sat up on the bed now and looked directly at Glenn.

He shook his head. "Like what?"

"She was murdered by the man she was having an affair with."

"So?" Then he lifted his eyebrows. "You think I might kill you?"

Lorraine got to her feet now and walked past him, towards the door. "No, of course not," she said. "You think I might kill you?" She didn't turn back to check his reaction, just lifted the handle on her bag and opened the door.

*

Down in reception, Glenn was checking out. He leaned on the desk and watched Lorraine while she stood looking at the pictures on the wall again. Done, he took his card from the girl behind the desk, noted how she hardly registered with him at all now, felt numb, felt how only yesterday he would have flirted with her, but now everything seemed muted.

He put his credit card away, shoving his wallet back into his coat pocket, and he walked over to Lorraine.

She sensed him approaching behind her and she cocked her head back slightly to speak to him. "See, this one?" she said, pointing at the dark picture she was gazing at.

"This is what the older woman here told me about."

Glenn leaned forward and peered at the picture. "What?" he asked. "I can't see anything."

"That there," she answered, her finger almost touching the picture now. "That was the house, see, and that's where we are now, where this hotel is now."

He leaned forward some more. "So, this hotel is built where that house used to be."

"Yeah, and see this?" she went on. "This is some guy, like a wizard or something, like a male witch."

"Yeah?"

"And he's doing this thing, see?"

"What thing?"

"Well, the woman here reckons that all around this place, around the house and down in the village, was being haunted by the dead girl, the one who..." She turned to look at him, then back to the picture again quickly. "Anyway, apparently the people who lived here then were so scared they'd stopped leaving their houses at night, so they asked this guy" – she tapped the picture with her finger – "to do something about it."

"And what did he do?"

"He got this fish from the river down there, right, and he, like, put the ghost in the fish." She turned to look at Glenn again.

"Eh?" he said.

They were standing looking at each other when the owner of the hotel came through reception again. She smiled at Lorraine and came over.

"Still looking at my pictures, I see," she said.

"Yeah," Lorraine answered. "I was just telling him about what you told me about the fish."

"Ah yes," the woman said. She turned to Glenn. "It's said the villagers were so afraid of the ghost that they went to the local sorcerer for help, and he agreed to lay the ghost."

"In a fish?" Glenn said.

The woman laughed. "I know it might sound strange, and I haven't heard of anything quite like it before, but yes, it's said he forced the ghost into the fish so it could only haunt the stream."

"And the haunting stopped?"

"That's what they say," the woman answered.

The three of them seemed to gaze together for a moment at the picture before Glenn said, "So, if the ghost was in the fish... where did it go then?"

"I'm sorry?" the woman said.

"Well, if the ghost was in the fish and it haunted the stream, what happened when the fish died? I mean, fish don't live that long. So what happened to the... ghost then?"

The woman frowned. "I'm no expert on things like that."

"I'm just thinking," Glenn went on, "If this... ghost had unfinished business – I mean, that's what they say ghosts hang around for, isn't it? There's something they still need to do, or tell someone or something, and if she did... then, when the fish died..."

The woman smirked. "I really don't know," she said. "The fish might not have lived out its life in the stream, it could have found its way back out to open water."

"Open water?"

"Well, yes, I think some fish only come to streams and rivers to spawn, then they go back out... but I really don't know..."

"So, the fish could have gone somewhere else and then died and she, I mean the ghost, would have found herself away from here somewhere and would have needed to find her way back here..."

The woman was frowning at him again now, her head pulled back slightly away from him. "Well, yes..." She hesitated. "But this is only a story. It's a local legend, that's all."

He looked at her sharply. "Yes, I know that," he snapped. "I was just thinking."

"Don't mind him," Lorraine said to the woman. "He's just a bit spooked by this whole ghost thing, aren't you? A bit... jumpy today. To be honest we didn't spend a very good night here the last time."

"Oh? I'm sorry to hear that. What was wrong? I like to keep my guests happy, so if there's something we could improve on..."

"Oh, no, the hotel's lovely, nice and old, very friendly receptionist. it's just... well, it was me, really. The first time we stayed here I... it sounds silly, but I thought I saw something, someone in the room, and then I was woken up by a noise."

"A noise?"

"Yeah, I don't know what it was, but it woke me."

The woman smiled. "We've been having some work done. It was probably that."

"Oh. What work?"

"Round the back. You know I told you we have a climbing wall and woodland walks. We're having some more of the area developed, to attract a few more for the outdoor pursuits, you know, it's big business."

"Oh, right, I see."

"We're not haunted," the woman said. "At least, not as far as I know. These little stories, you know, they are fascinating, and then you're sleeping in one of the rooms and you start to think more about it and before you know it you think you've seen something... the brain is a great deceiver."

"Are you saying we imagined it?" Glenn asked.

"Well, I just..."

"Because I know what I see. I'm straight up. I know what's right in front of my eyes."

"I just wouldn't want it to have put you off staying with us again," the woman said.

"Oh, yeah," Glenn answered, "I bet you wouldn't. Anything to keep the customers coming, eh? Anything to keep business healthy. Don't bother telling them the bloody place is bloody haunted!"

"I really don't think..."

"Yeah? Well, I do." Then he turned to Lorraine. "Come on," he said, "let's get out of here."

*

The sky had cleared itself of dusty clouds and it stretched out blue like a sun-filled ocean. Lorraine got into the car beside Glenn and she looked up out of the windscreen. As he started the engine and the car moved slowly over the car park and out of the gates for the hotel, Lorraine felt the low winter sun target her eyes and burn. Glenn pulled down his visor and cursed, but Lorraine just closed her eyes and felt her smile spread on her face. He was spooked. He was so spooked. It was perfect really. The timing couldn't be better. It was like a new beginning. Like the world was opening up for her. Fresh with possibility. Like there was nothing she couldn't do. And she'd do it partly for Sarah, though mostly for herself of course.

They took the road up and away from the village, over the top of the hill, where Anne had once walked to her mother's, once walked with Bess by her side and a baby heavy in her womb. The road swayed, the sky low and rocks and boulders scattered on the land at either side of them.

They'd both been silent since they got in the car, like an unspoken deal, or like their voices were scared of speaking these events, or like there were no words they could think of that would cover the last couple of hours.

"That was weird," Glenn said at last.

"Yeah."

"I mean that was really weird."

"It was," Lorraine answered. "But I told you when we were here before that something was going on."

He turned to look at her quickly then back to the road in front of him. "Yeah."

"But you never listen."

"What?"

"You. You never listen to me, you never take any notice of what I say."

"I do."

"No, you don't, you..."

"Christ, let's not argue about that now! What about what just happened? Aren't you freaked out? 'Cause I know I am."

Lorraine was quiet for a minute. When she spoke again, it was calmly and carefully measured. "I was freaked out the first time we came here, remember? But you said I was dreaming or imagining or just stupid."

"I never said you were stupid."

"Yes, you did, you..."

"Why the hell are we arguing about this? I just saw a ghost. A fucking ghost!"

"And I saw one last time and you didn't believe me!"

They were quiet again for a minute and Lorraine sat and looked out of the window, her face turned away from Glenn.

"I never said you were stupid," he said quietly.

"Well, if you didn't say it, you thought it."

"No, I didn't."

"I know you did. That's what you think of me, you think I'm stupid. Stupid tart. Stupid cow. Well, we'll see about that."

He turned to her sharply again, one eye still on the road.

"What's that supposed to mean?" he asked.

"I meant what I said about Julia."

"What?"

"How come she gets all the fancy clothes and the big house and the money? What do I get?"

"You do alright."

"Alright isn't good enough."

"What are you saying?"

"I'm saying I'm not gonna be fucked over like Sarah Vernon. I'm not gonna be fooled by some man. I want my share. I want what I deserve, and if you don't give it to me I'm telling Julia all about what you get up to when you're with me."

A Bad Winter

Derbyshire, 1760s

When it happened she felt all things had fallen away and only the burning was left. She felt the trees and the earth and the cold air and every other living thing was gone, or they were hazy and paper-thin and so unimportant to her. She existed in a strange bubble where she seemed incapable of tasting or experiencing anything that was not connected to him. Joseph. Joseph Bradshaw. He was all that mattered. Not her mother and father or any of the people she knew. Not food or sleep or her own wellbeing. She didn't think of anything else. Only him.

When that happened, Sarah followed the way she felt. She followed her own body and her own heart, to Joseph. Again and again. This odd state she was in was a kind of sickness, a type of madness. She lay with him in the outdoors, up amongst the trees behind his house, while his wife sat inside by the fire. Sarah felt nothing at all about his wife or anyone else for that matter. It was like her feeling for Joseph was so huge there was no room for anyone or anything else inside of her. She wanted him again and again. She felt a need on her skin to feel him, like her own nerve endings craved only him, her sense of smell only his, her eyes his image, her ears his voice. Nothing else would do. When he left her side and walked away it was as if he was killing her.

She would let him do anything. And she would do anything for him.

She would give him her whole life.

*

When that happened everything within and without of Sarah denied it. It was pure love, her and him. She loved him. He loved her. Or else why would it feel the way it did? How could that be? It was beyond the cold earth and the white sky and the understanding of any person.

The trance-like state she had lived in for the last few months altered, but it didn't alter by much. Her eyes still felt hooded. Her body weak. Her brain confused. Her voice silenced. Her ears bewildered. Only now, the reason for all of this was not physically there. Sarah couldn't find Joseph. She now experienced a heaviness she had never experienced before. And still only one thing mattered. Maybe more now than ever.

At first she was aware of the heaviness on her body. It was cold and dark where she was without him. She stayed in the darkness and hoped to feel him near her soon, but he didn't come. After some time she heard Bess and her cold body ached all the more for Joseph because of it. The dog barked and whimpered a little. And there was a scratching. Somewhere, near to Sarah, Bess was clawing. Bess's hot breath in the cold air, her feet on the cold damp ground like hands on dough. Bess was close to Sarah now. But so was someone else. Someone who was sketchy to Sarah. Someone who she never allowed into her sight or her thoughts at all. Anne. Joseph's wife. She was there. Sarah could hear her. She spoke in the darkness, a muffled sound somewhere out of Sarah's reach. Sarah heard her voice and then Sarah felt a struggle come over her. The need to find Joseph was stronger than ever then. A compulsion. As necessary as her arms and legs. At first she still couldn't see anything, but she willed herself to move. And then she was by the house. And from there she looked everywhere she knew for him. There were people, but Sarah was only aware of them as she was aware of the distant hills and the broken faraway clouds and the passing of any time at all anymore. She moved as if she was cloaked in mist, heavy with worry, slowed by age. She went by the Low Drop, over the road and back again, not getting too close to the window for fear the men would see her, but close enough to hear him if he was there. Then up at Inkerswell's house, where she knew Joseph had been. She followed the memory of his footsteps, his scent still in the air and clinging to the ground around the building. Right up to the house and to the kitchen window. But she couldn't find him there either. Other places she lingered, and moved around in the village, but there was no sign of Joseph.

Sarah had the strange feeling that she would do this

forever. And then something changed.

One night she felt her body pressed upon from all about her. Like she had been when she had first heard Bess in the darkness, and Joseph's wife. But different. Now she felt herself constricted like she hadn't been before. And looking for Joseph was impossible. Sarah couldn't move. She felt defeated for a while. She felt love had finally crushed her.

Once, she would have looked to the water as a way out of her misery. At one time, if she had lived, Sarah would have hoped to die in its depths rather than stay in the world without Joseph. Now she found herself freed from it and water all around her. Still, there was only one place she wished to be.

Today

"You're talking crazy."

"Am I?"

She could see him looking at her fast every moment or so, his eyes flitting back to the road and then back to check her face. He was wondering if she meant it.

They rounded the corner onto Lorraine's street. Glenn drove slowly past her house, meaning to turn the car around in the cul-de-sac at the top.

"Is that...?"

Lorraine followed his gaze as they passed her front door. Parked on the front of the house was the familiar old Vauxhall her husband drove, rusty on the edges and dingy with dirt.

"Yeah, he's in. Drop me at the top here."

Glenn turned the car in the cul-de-sac and came to a slow stop.

"Lorraine." He leaned towards her, but she was already pulling at the door handle to let herself out.

"I meant what I said, Glenn," she answered. She opened the door and swung her legs out of the car. Then she turned her body a little to speak to him. "It's about time you started taking notice of what I say, today should have shown you that. I only say things I mean, Glenn."

She slammed the door shut and walked away down the street. She was only a few paces from the car when she heard the engine start up again, rev fiercely, and the car come fast up behind her. Lorraine just reached the other side of the road from the cul-de-sac when she looked quickly behind her to see Glenn's car at her back. She stepped onto the pavement and the car skidded in the road as it sped off. She stopped for just a second, and slowed her breathing. "Tosser," she muttered under her breath.

*

Glenn could feel the pressure inside his head throb like a pulse in a squeezed thumb. He needed to get away from her. He needed to get out of here. He needed to get home. To Julia. He

164

thought about going home right now and telling Julia everything. That would be the way. Get in there first. Don't give Lorraine the chance to mess his life up. Don't give the bitch the chance to mess with him. He'd get in there first and tell Julia everything, and then what could Lorraine do? Nothing. She'd be powerless. He smiled to himself as he thought about taking that power from her. Then he gripped the steering wheel hard as he thought about Julia, her face if he told her all this, how angry she'd be, what she'd say, what she'd do. She'd leave him, he was sure and she'd take everything she could. Take him to the cleaners. Bleed him dry. She was that sort of woman. Bloody women. Which of them weren't that sort? It was all they wanted. Money. What they could get. Bloody thieving women. No, he couldn't tell Julia.

Glenn relaxed a little as his brain began to sort through his options and settle itself into the groove of a plan. By the time he drove into the long, gravel drive and up to the house, the outbuildings and the stretch of land to the left where Julia's Springer Spaniel ran and sniffed the earth, Glenn had decided how he was going to put a stop to Lorraine's nonsense.

*

They met in the pub two days later. Lorraine couldn't remember a single time they'd ever met in a pub before. Except that first time, of course. Except the first time they ever met when he slid up to her at the bar and insisted on buying the drinks she was getting for her and a friend. He'd stood there and opened his wallet, his free hand gently pushing hers back down onto the bar. "Please, allow me," he'd said with mock chivalry. He had her instantly. The woman she was with was someone she spoke to now and then outside the school gates, but she didn't care for the friendship and would much rather stand and chat with this clearly well-off man who was buying the drinks right now. She'd ditched the other woman, and that had been that. Sold. But they'd never arranged to meet in a pub again.

Lorraine was thinking this as she pushed the heavy door and let the smell of beer and the low chatter and the clink of stray glasses waft over her. Why did he want to meet in a pub? It signalled a shift, she was sure of that. A distance, maybe an end to something, but she didn't care about that. Why should she care?

She glanced around her, but couldn't see him, so she walked up to the bar and scanned the pumps in front of her. He'd chosen a dingy pub. Real ale on the pumps and a portly old man behind the bar. An old man pub. Why the hell had he brought her here? Lorraine felt a sigh fall into her middle as the old man waited, his arms stretched out, his hands on beloved pumps, and she read the names of the beers in front of her.

"I'll have a half of that blonde one there," she said.

The barman nodded and grabbed a glass. "You know it's cheaper to buy a pint," he said.

Lorraine was fiddling in her purse for change. She looked up. His face was slightly red, blotchy where his stubble poked through on his cheeks. "I don't want a pint," she answered.

She looked around her while she gathered some stray money from her purse. A large mirror on one wall to the right. Artwork on the other. Dark wood tables with beer mats and an unlit candle and menus for food. It was quiet in here. Glenn had asked her to meet him in a quiet old man pub, as opposed to a busier, louder one uptown. It struck her that he didn't want an audience. He wanted it to be public but not so public that someone might stick their nose in.

She looked around again. He was over there. Sitting with his back to her, staring out the window. She recognised his hair and the way he held himself. His shoulders, even the collar of his shirt folded over the neck of his jumper. It could only be him. No one else.

Lorraine paid for the beer and walked over to where he sat. She pushed the chair opposite him out with her leg and he got up. He leaned forward and kissed her awkwardly on the cheek. The whole thing was like it wasn't her and it wasn't him. Like they hardly knew each other. Like he'd never lain with her and didn't know every inch of her skin. Like they'd never kissed or slept with their arms thrown over the other's warm body.

Lorraine sat down and took a gulp of the beer. She noticed Glenn's pint was three quarters drunk already. He'd been early. Or he'd drunk fast.

"So, why did you want to meet here?" she asked.

Glenn held his hands tightly around his pint and looked down, like he was thinking over his words, like he knew he had to say them but struggled with how they'd sound. Lorraine had the sudden strange feeling she was losing something. A rumble of panic entered her chest. The weirdest thing. Something ending. And this wasn't how it was supposed to go. This wasn't how she'd planned it at all.

"I thought we should... meet somewhere public," he answered.

"Why?"

He looked up at her then and Lorraine saw a vague twitch to the corner of his mouth. Then one of his hands left the pint glass and fumbled on the seat beside him. He picked up an envelope and put it on the table next to Lorraine's beer.

"I'm gonna be busy over the next few weeks," he said.

Lorraine looked down at the envelope, thick with paper, then back up at his face. "What?"

"I've got a lot on, so take this."

Lorraine grabbed the envelope.

"Don't open it here," he said. He caught her hand on the envelope across the table quickly and he looked around in a low panic. Lorraine followed his eyes, but there were only two other people in there, and they looked half asleep "Just... I hope that... settles things," he said. He downed his pint and got up to leave. Lorraine's hand was still on the envelope and she watched as he stood. She had a feeling she hadn't had for years, not since she was a teenager and Martyn dumped her after two months, or when Lee held her on the back seat of the bus and whispered sweet words that made her insides surge, only to turn up with someone new the following week. Lorraine looked up at Glenn as he stood and she felt like that girl all over again. He was leaving her. He was saying it was over. Not in so many words. He hadn't said it, but she could feel it as clear as she could feel the wind. She just stared at him. This unexpected feeling growing inside her body – she wasn't supposed to care. Why did she care?

Glenn put the empty pint glass down on the table and picked his coat up from the back of the seat. He stepped away from the chair and hesitated for just a second.

"See you soon," he said.

*

Lorraine had sat there quite still for a few minutes after he'd gone. She felt like all the liquid in her body had stopped and her face was frozen with a weird tension. Then her heart began to beat faster than felt safe and she could hear it loud in her own head and ears. She picked up the glass in front of her and drank the beer down in one gulp. Then she took the envelope and placed it on her lap. With the table as a screen, she pulled apart the envelope carefully and placed her finger inside to open it just a fraction. Inside the envelope was a stack of money. She didn't know how much but it looked like a lot. Strangely, the sight of this much money didn't move her at all. She wondered for a quick second what the hell was wrong with her, but then the drag in her middle took over her brain and she felt the discomfort of the looks of the other two people and the barman firmly on her.

Lorraine felt an uncontrollable heat fill her face. She pushed the envelope into her bag quickly and stood up. He'd chosen this pub carefully. She could see that now. It was public but quiet, the perfect place to meet someone who might make a scene. You couldn't exactly kick off in a pub like this.

Out in the street she found her mind going over the words he'd used and trying to figure them into something she could understand.

See you soon. What did that mean? What had just happened? This wasn't what she'd planned. This wasn't how it was supposed to be at all.

*

Two days later she could hardly stand the way this felt. She'd

168

lain awake at night with everything he'd said and the way he'd looked a constant tumble in her mind. She got up that morning and felt a fierce anger building in her body. Who did he think he was? Tosser. Did he think he could just pay her off? Pay her a couple of grand and she would shut up and go away? He was messing with the wrong woman. She felt this sting of anger and then a sharpness of loss again, so strong it doubled her over in physical pain. It continued in this way, anger and tears, until Lorraine felt she couldn't stand it any longer. She had to do something.

*

Glenn's house wasn't hard to find, even though she'd never been there before. Two minutes online with only his name and the city, and she found his address easily. She'd called a taxi and then spoken Glenn's postcode through the clear divider between herself and the driver. He'd nodded and typed the postcode into his satnav. It was so easy.

When they reached the bottom of the driveway, the taxi driver asked Lorraine if she wanted him to take her all the way up to the house. Lorraine stared at the tall hedges and the secluded driveway and said no. She didn't want to announce herself openly. She wanted to be a complete surprise. Lorraine got out of the taxi and walked slowly to the foot of the drive. Once on the other side of those tall hedges she looked up at the house.

The driveway swooped around to the right in the shape of a spoon. Up there at the top, where it expanded to allow more than one car to turn, was a large water feature, like something you'd see abroad, Lorraine thought. Like nothing she'd ever seen at the front of a house in real life before.

Beneath her feet, the driveway was made up of millions of cream-coloured stones. As she walked on them, her feet constantly slipped, and she soon realised this drive wasn't meant to be walked on, was never walked on, because the people who came here all drove up and only got out of their cars at the top where the stones stopped and the perfectly-laid paving began.

Lorraine paused about halfway up the drive and

looked at the buildings now rising with the land in front of her. It was obviously a converted farm of some sort. The house was stone-built and old, but with new PVC windows and a conservatory on the end. The field swooped out to the right and behind, and in an L shape; the buildings at the far end were high but not lived in, not containing the windows and doors of a home.

Lorraine walked a little closer to the house, and the cottage-style windows and tied-back floral curtains were enough alone to make the anger bubble in her again. A couple of grand. Against all this. He'd paid her off with a couple of grand and Julia got all this.

As she reached the edge of the house she took in the two cars sitting on the level drive. One was Glenn's car. Lorraine recognised it straight away. She should, she'd spent enough time in it. The other one was a 4x4 which Lorraine presumed belonged to Julia. Lorraine stared at the vehicle and felt a stab of jealousy low down in her middle. She'd never met the woman, but already Lorraine went from hating her to pitying her and back again so fast she felt like if she did meet her she wouldn't be able to control any of it.

She thought about that then. As if she'd not considered it before. Julia would probably be here. Julia was more likely to be here than Glenn. It would most likely be Julia Lorraine came into contact with first. She couldn't imagine the meeting though. Not really. It seemed so beyond her understanding she couldn't picture it at all.

*

The front door opened and the sudden sound of people and their lives was released into the cold mid-morning. Julia kissed Glenn on the cheek and then turned quickly and strode towards the car. Lorraine ducked back beside the house, her face poking around the side of the old stone building just enough to see Julia get into the 4x4 and start the engine. She'd kissed him, her warm mouth touching his skin, as if everything was fine. In that simple moment Lorraine hated Julia. Glenn had already closed the door before the 4x4 was away from the front of the house, and Lorraine pushed herself back beside the stone as Julia drove down the bumpy drive and away.

She left it a few minutes before she made her way around the house and to the front door. She passed the cottage-style window and looked briefly inside. Julia had really gone to town with the farmhouse theme, by the looks of things. Probably imagined it symbolised country living. Probably thought it meant she was better than everyone else. A pinewood table sat in the middle of the kitchen and, to the right, Lorraine could see a Welsh dresser. Beside that, on the wall, an old sword of some sort was mounted and held on, its handle like a circular metal cage. Above it, an old photograph and a plaque. Julia really had got into this whole old English cottage thing, Lorraine thought. Daft cow.

The mid-morning air was still cold enough to show Lorraine's breath, though the snow had all disappeared and the ground was only damp. She stopped at the front door and watched her own air leave her body. She hated him. She hated her. Who did he think he was anyway? Or her? Carrying on as if nothing had happened. Lorraine wasn't having that. She wasn't about to crawl away quietly and let it go like that.

She brought her hand up to the door in a closed fist and knocked hard. Glenn opened the door fast with a smile on his face, which soon fell. He'd obviously expected it to be Julia, come back because she'd forgotten something.

"Lorraine," he said. "What...?"

"Aren't you going to ask me in?"

"How did you know...? I mean, how did you find...?"

Lorraine smiled and felt the upper hand she had in that moment lift her. "Oh, come on, Glenn, it isn't difficult to find anyone's address these days, you know that."

Glenn's face had lost some colour and his mouth twitched again at one side like it had in the pub.

"But I thought..."

"You thought we were quits?" Lorraine pushed forward and entered the kitchen, shoving Glenn to one side slightly. He looked stunned for a minute. Then he closed the door behind them.

"What do you want, Lorraine?"

"Well, for a start I wanted to see where you live. With her. I wanted to see who you are."

Glenn held his arms out by his sides, his palms upturned, to indicate everything around him. "Well, here you are, you've seen it," he said.

"Yeah," she said. "Pretty nice."

She swept her eyes around the room. The solid, wooden dresser, holding plates as a display, probably expensive plates, she thought. The matching kettle, toaster and breadbin. The sword on the wall.

"Lorraine," Glenn said. "I don't know what you think..."

She held up her hand. "What's that?" she asked. "An antique?"

Glenn turned to look behind him. He took the sword from the wall and weighed it in his hands. "Family heirloom," he answered. "Been in my family, I don't know... a bloody long time, though."

"Worth a lot?"

He looked up at her, holding the sword a little more firmly now. "What? I don't know. It supposedly went down the male side of my family until my great-great-great whatever, granddad, and then it passed to my mum's side. I don't know what it's worth. Why do you want to know?"

Lorraine shrugged, an over-emphasised look of not caring on her face. "Just thinking how much money you must have tied up here."

Glenn eyed her for a minute, trying to figure out what she was doing. "What's this all about, Lorraine?" he said. "What do you want?"

"Did you really think a couple of grand was gonna do it? Did you think I'd just go away quietly and leave you alone for a couple of grand?"

"What?"

"You used me!"

Lorraine had promised herself she wouldn't let emotion come within an inch of her voice and her mind and

172

her body at all. But she felt it now anyway. She heard her own words come out of her mouth louder than she'd meant, more forceful and full of accusation.

"You just used me!"

"We used each other!" he answered.

She was shaking her head, knowing it was stupid to argue with him, knowing she couldn't blame him really for saying that. But in the end she'd felt something. And he hadn't.

She looked up at him now. There was a creak somewhere else in the house. A loose floorboard or a swollen door. A waft of breeze or hot-water pipes shifting. They both glanced at the ceiling. Then back at each other.

"It's an old house," he said.

"Yeah," she answered. "Old, and worth a packet."

*

She'd looked for him. She'd been back to all the places she'd known him. Over time things changed, buildings, the land, people, animals, vehicles, but Sarah remained the same. When she looked she found traces of a life she'd once known. A smell, a person's hair, the way someone walked and the things they said. Sarah observed all these things from a strange, muffled existence. She followed the only trace of Joseph she could find. She held the thread and she walked with the people who carried something of him within themselves.

Sarah spent much of this time in confusion, but when she felt herself close to her love again and she felt the power of all she had once known with him, nothing else seemed to matter. It was a sickness. It was a madness. Love was a madness, and what else could it be?

She was aware, in some way, of things not being as they should be. The place she was in. The people she was with. The people she found were never Joseph, but they held a part of him inside themselves somewhere. It was a piece of hope. She kept following the hope.

She followed it through babies. Sarah felt a sadness so heavy she thought it would hold her to the ground. There was no one in the world she would rather have had a baby with than Joseph. Babies are the result of love. They are what comes of two people's union, their hearts together. But the babies she followed were not born of love. They each held a sticky strand of Joseph in their bodies. But they did not hold any love from him. They were born out of convenience and coincidence and situation and happenstance. Sarah followed these children who had Joseph's eyes and the same turn of their heads. She watched them.

*

She had come to this place now, where the wind circled the buildings, just like it had once done at Hill Head House. She had found this place where the walls held conversations from previous inhabitants like the sea holds salt. She felt herself drift in this house, and she felt herself so close to all she had wanted now.

They were both here.

She could feel the same thing in the air she had felt between herself and Joseph. She moved. She could hear their voices. Some pain. Some fear. She moved closer to them.

*

He was shaking his head, looking down at the sword as he moved it from one hand to the other.

"What do you want, Lorraine?"

"What do I want?" she shouted. "Oh let me see. All of it." She swept her arm around in the space that circled her.

Glenn held his head back a little and snorted out a laugh. "You're crazy," he said. He pointed at her with the sword held out in front of him now. There was something in her eyes. Something he'd never seen in her before. It made him nervous. She was serious about this, wasn't she? She wouldn't let this go.

"Yeah?" she said. She took a step towards him, her neck pushed forward so that her head jutted. Then she reached out and grabbed the sword in his hand. "You have no idea how crazy I am."

They both held on. She was close up to him now, the

174

sword held tight between them, blade upwards and pointing at the ceiling.

"Just calm down now, Lorraine." There was a warning in his voice, though he was still shouting and it was held under his anger.

She was pushing against him, her hand grasping the handle of the sword along with his. "Calm down?" she shouted back. "I won't fucking calm down. You try to pay me off with two fucking grand, shut me up with that, while she gets all this!"

"Do you really care that much about money?"

She stared hard into his eyes. The way he'd always been able to talk her into anything. The way she folded so easily at a simple word from him. The way it had felt when she'd been with him. The way it felt when he got up and walked away. Feelings she'd never recognised or looked closely enough at. She pushed the handle of the sword hard against his stomach and he folded slightly.

"I never cared about the money!" she screamed at him. "I cared about you!"

He pushed back against her now and she felt the cold metal of the sword's handle too brutal.

"What are you talking about?" He leaned his face closer to hers to emphasis his words. "We were fuck buddies. That's all."

It felt like he was killing her. It felt like those words were reaching forward into her and taking her life. And she was fighting. When the rage filled all the spaces inside Lorraine she felt something else in the room there with her. She didn't take her eyes off Glenn, his words still ripping at her insides, and she saw him flash a glance behind her and his face change, the colour leave him and the fear take its place in a second. His grasp on the sword loosened as his attention was pulled to the sight behind Lorraine. The sight he'd seen before that day down by the stream outside the hotel. The girl. The dead girl. He let go of the sword as he looked into her face again, and Lorraine's anger at his betrayal of her body pushed her forward. As Glenn let go all the tension between them was released and passed fully to Lorraine. They had been holding the sword between them, blade up and now, sword still firmly in her hand, Lorraine felt it jerk to the side as Glenn let go. Like it had a life of its own. Like she wasn't in control of it at all. The blade swiped at Glenn's middle before Lorraine dropped it.

Derbyshire, 1760s

He was hanged two days after Anne had seen him last. Anne had been to see him only the once and he'd spoken words to her that made him feel lighter once they had left his body. Not much is said straight in life, he thought, but when facing death or disaster all the plain speaking seemed to lay itself flat and it was right then.

Joseph had made his peace with God. It had been an accident. He knew that. He was sure God did too. He wished through every moment of every day since it happened that he could change it, go back and do everything differently, make it so it never happened. That one small passing of time by the wall when she died. If he could change that... but now he would face what was to come. Maybe he wouldn't see Sarah again. And he was frightened of what lay on the other side. But this was his fate now.

Joseph was hanged. He remembered seeing the people waiting to watch as he approached. He made it so that his mind didn't register who any of them were. He made himself unsee them. Though he knew Anne was there and he could hear her wail and cry, he wouldn't look at her. He remembered the feel of the rope as it was looped and tightened around his neck. The shouting from the crowd. He could hear the noise, but words were useless things. He seemed to live only inside his own head at that time. He saw the sky, white-bright with clouds of blue beneath the sheen. He thought spring would come soon. He thought about the changing of the seasons and how it affected life, the work to be done in the fields that he wouldn't be there to do, bright mornings, light evenings, calves being born and flowers growing. Then he was aware of movement. Then the drop. The awful, terrifying drop. And the panic. He remembered the terrible weight of his own body, the pain his torso and his limbs caused him, the feeling of great pressure in his head, pushing up, all of him inside his head at that moment, pushing. Then he seemed to forget his arms and legs and his torso, he seemed to forget he ever had a body at all. He couldn't say if the pain had gone or if he just became unaware of it. Then he was cut down.

*

Aaron had watched with a deep sickness in his stomach and an acid in his mouth. He'd watched as Joseph was brought before them to be hanged and he'd felt, at the very least, complicit, at the worst, responsible. The burden of being the one who'd told all that he'd seen, the one who had seen it in the first place and then had directed his pointed finger at Joseph, was heavier than he could ever have imagined. He'd done right. It must have been the right thing to do. Though his mother's words seemed to come back to his ears more and more lately. *See all and say nowt.* His mother wouldn't have told. She'd have kept the knowledge inside of her, perhaps to use at a later time, when it could benefit her or someone else. She wouldn't have supposed herself to be the one to say who was right and wrong, who was good and evil, who should live or die.

But Aaron wasn't like his mother. His mother had been truly wise and knew things, he didn't know how. Aaron didn't know things. He just watched people and what they did and listened to what they said. He knew about the nature his mother had taught him. How to stop sickness. How to help fever. What to do when someone bled. But he couldn't see anyone's future rightly. He couldn't cause a love that wasn't there. He couldn't deal with spirits and the dead.

He stood with everyone else waiting to see the evil Joseph Bradshaw hang for murdering Sarah Vernon, and he had no idea what was right or wrong anymore. This was supposed to be the right thing. Death for death. But this felt wrong.

The crowd were shouting and jeering when Joseph's body dropped and his arms and legs worked frantically to find a way to be free. Beside Aaron, Anne cried out, unable to stay quiet and calm any longer. Aaron looked to the ground. He felt a shame like he never had before. He took from his pocket the posy he had prepared, and he supported the weakness of Anne as her body crumbled. He held the posy before her nose and told her to hold herself strong. The scent was known to

Aaron to revive the kind of faintness he could see in Anne. And he'd predicted this would happen. He let himself be a place of comfort for Anne. He looked upwards and saw the sheet-white sky break like cloth, revealing the blue of spring beneath it. Too early, he thought, the year was too young yet for any sign of spring.

When Joseph was cut down and the people began to move away, Aaron stayed. He watched Anne kneel by the body of her husband while she could, before he was to be taken away. This would all be dealt with quickly, Aaron knew. They would take the body to the boundary of the village and they would find a place to bury him as quickly as they could.

Aaron told Anne he would go with her husband. She looked up at him then and, maybe for the first time during this whole bad business, he felt he was making some kind of amends. He saw the gratefulness in her eyes, the way she appreciated this one, late act. He would go and he would see that Joseph's body was dealt with respectfully.

He began to suspect something was amiss as he travelled with the other men and the body of Joseph Bradshaw to the boundary of their village. Aaron had seen dead men before. Men and women. And this man in front of him now did not look like the others. He eyed the men with him to see if anyone else felt the prickle of life right there that he did. No one met Aaron's eyes, and they either didn't see or feel or suspect anything or they just wanted this man buried no matter what.

After several moments had passed, Aaron leaned forward to the flesh of Joseph and touched him.

"What are yer doing?" It was the constable.

Aaron felt the beat of a pulse faintly in Joseph's neck and he looked up and into the constable's eyes.

"He's not dead," he said.

"What do yer say?" the constable asked. "This man were 'anged. 'E is dead."

"He's not dead," Aaron continued. "I can feel the life in him. He's not dead."

The constable stared for a moment at Aaron's face,

then at the body before him. He ordered the horses to be stopped and he called Inkerswell to him.

"What is it?" Inkerswell asked.

"Sir, there is uncertainty."

"What do yer say?"

Aaron faced Inkerswell. "The man is still alive," he said.

"What? He can't be alive. We saw him hang."

Aaron lowered himself to the face of Joseph again. He placed his cheek close to Joseph's nose and he closed his eyes. He waited there for a moment then he stood up straight and faced the two men again.

"There are signs of life," he said.

He took the posy from his belt and he held it a couple of inches from Joseph's face.

*

When he felt the life enter him again and he became aware of his body once more, the pain he felt shooting in his extremities was almost worse than the death he thought he'd endured already. It was the worst pain he'd ever experienced. Life as cruel and sharp as any weapon flashing back into every corner of his arms and legs. He felt himself move. Then slowly, Joseph felt his body return to some normality. He looked around him and he saw the sky, dark over the hills with heavy rain to come, so changeable yet. Then he took in the sight of the men standing about him.

"What'll we do with 'im?" the constable asked.

Inkerswell just stared down at the body of Joseph Bradshaw, very much alive, and seemed dumbfounded.

"He survived the rope," Aaron said. "That's a sign."

"A sign of what?" Inkerswell asked.

"That he is not for death yet."

"But 'e is guilty," the constable said. "If 'e is not to meet 'is death, then what?"

Inkerswell still pulled the thoughts through his brain. He looked up at Aaron. "You say he is not to die for this crime?"

"It isn't I who says it," Aaron answered. "You see

180

him. He was hanged before all of us, and yet he lives."

"Tis the devil then."

"No," Aaron said. "It's not the devil who reprieves a man at death."

Inkerswell fell silent again. He looked down at Joseph. He'd always been a strong man. Tall, his body built for hard work, but plenty of men of his size had died by the rope. He took a deep breath and puffed out his chest.

"Transportation," he said. "There is nothing else. He cannot live a free man amongst us. He shall be branded and transported to the new world. There he'll find hard work the like of which he's never known. And if this is God's will, so be it."

"So what do we do now?" the constable asked.

Inkerswell turned to face him, his cheeks red with his frustration and confusion, desperately trying to regain control of this situation. "You go back and tell them as asks that all is well," he said. "You tell them Bradshaw is buried here this day." Then he pointed at the constable. "You never speak of this."

The constable nodded mutely and turned to go.

"And you and I," Inkerswell said to Aaron, "we shall deal with this unfortunate business, and we shall never utter a single word about it for as long as we live, not to anyone else and not to each other, you understand?"

Aaron nodded and dipped his head slightly.

"It will be as if this never happened," he went on. "I know you are comfortable with concealing truths, and this one you shall take to your grave."

Today

Something happened then. Sarah felt all the anger from Lorraine. All the love and the wanting and the need for love. All of it growing and tumbling. She felt it all building and moving towards the one same end as always. Death. That was the only point of life. Sarah felt a rush of disorientation. She had lived in colour once, when she was with Joseph. Her days had been bright and she'd imagined a future with him. She'd sorted this imagined future in her head. She'd placed herself in his house, by his side, having his babies and growing old with him. She'd had a future then.

Then he had gone and she had found herself in darkness. No other dreams to take the place of the ones she'd had before. No other future to imagine. So she'd followed her love and she'd tried to find her way back to him. Then an even stranger thing had happened. Sarah had found herself constricted by another form. And she had existed like this, moving through water, cold and held in. When she was released from this strange experience she continued to look for her love. She never found him.

Sarah seemed to come fully to where she was now. She saw the blood of this man in front of her ink through his clothes. The same blood that had once pulsed through Joseph's body. And with it she felt a rush of Joseph and she saw clearly for the first time all that had happened.

He had almost died. But he hadn't. He had almost died because of Sarah's death, but he had survived and instead had made a journey across the sea to another land. Sarah saw him as a shadow leaving. She saw that he thought of her sometimes. But not in the same way she thought of him. Sarah was consumed by Joseph. Joseph was troubled by Sarah. He had loved her lightly. He had only loved her to a point, and no further. If she'd lived he would have killed her anyway and forced her to into a living death.

But she would never hurt any piece of him. She felt herself move. The disorientation was gone now and she felt as clear as the opening of spring after a bad winter.

*

Lorraine had looked down at her own hands, one still holding the sword, one pressed against his stomach. She realised she had instinctively pulled the sword away from him as soon as it had met his flesh. A quick action she hadn't even been aware of as she did it. Now she looked down and saw her own hand becoming sticky with Glenn's blood. She dropped the sword to the ground and it clattered with a high chime on the stone kitchen floor.

"Oh shit oh shit oh shit. Glenn. Glenn."

He was holding onto her shoulder with one hand, his other pushed into the wound. Lorraine's head began to spin and become light as she stepped away from him.

"Oh God oh God. What do I do?"

"Call a fucking ambulance!"

Lorraine took her mobile from her pocket and watched her fingers try to navigate the numbers on the touchscreen, her hands shaking so much she felt they were no longer her own.

She made the call, her voice sounding too high and frantic in her own head. "Hurry!" she'd shouted.

"How did it happen?" the voice on the other end asked. And she'd heard the sobs reaching the back of her throat and spilling out into her words. "Just hurry up. Please!"

At the hospital she'd waited while he was seen and treated. She felt her whole body crumble when the doctor told her he'd be fine.

"It's a nasty wound, but not deep enough to have done him any serious damage. He was lucky, it could have been worse with a weapon like that," the doctor said. "We've patched him up, but you should be more careful in future when you're cleaning old weapons like that. Could be dangerous."

She'd stared at the doctor and then nodded. "Yes," she answered. "Yes, of course."

"Well, you can see him now."

Lorraine walked into the room. His eyes were already on her as if he'd been waiting all along for her to walk through the door.

"I'm so sorry, Glenn, I didn't mean to do it. It was an accident."

He kept his eyes on her. He let go a long breath. "That's what I told them," he said. "An accident. Said we were cleaning it, the sword."

"Yeah, the doctor just mentioned that. Do you think they believed you?"

He shrugged. "I don't know, probably not, but it doesn't matter, does it?"

"Glenn..."

"About what happened," he went on. "In the kitchen." He tried to lean forward and lowered his voice. "I saw her." he said. "The girl. I saw her again. She was right there in the kitchen, just before you..."

Then he leaned back against the pillows again, pain stopping him.

Lorraine was sitting on the edge of the bed next to him. She took his hand. She'd wanted to say... what did she want to say? She loved him? It was too ridiculous. It was too stupid. Out of the question. And yet...

"Glenn. All that stuff I said about the money, you know I didn't mean that, you know..."

"Did you see her?" he asked.

"What?"

"The girl. Is that what happened? Did you see her and... the shock... and you were holding the sword... is that why?"

She stared at him. "It all happened so fast," she said.

He nodded. "Yes, I know, and that's what I'll tell Julia. I've been thinking about it. We'll say someone tried to break in, but I was there, and there was a ... scuffle, but it all happened so fast. And then they ran off when they knew they'd injured me..."

Lorraine watched his face, his mind working out how best to lay this in front of Julia, what to tell her so she didn't suspect a thing, how to protect her, how to keep her. And she realised he'd never give that much thought to her, Lorraine. She'd always be what she'd always been, and he'd never strive to protect her and keep her. He could let her go. It only took two grand. As easy as that.

*

She'd recognise Julia anywhere. She'd only seen her once, leaving the house and getting into her 4x4 while Lorraine hid round the side of the wall. Only that few moments, but she'd never forget what she looked like. How could she forget the woman she'd lost out to? Oh, he was a dog alright. Glenn. She knew perfectly well. He was a total dog, but love falls where it falls. It isn't perfect. It isn't even. It isn't fair.

Julia was going into the hospital and Lorraine was leaving. They exchanged the same air for two seconds as they passed just inside reception. But Julia would never know. Lorraine couldn't help thinking it was better for her that way. It was better for Lorraine. It was better to walk away and leave things tidy.

As she was leaving, Lorraine passed the little café area in reception. Small Formica tables and spindly chairs. Plastic coffee cups and wooden stirrers. People sitting with worry for company, and sadness and fear. Lorraine looked at the people. People who loved someone. People who'd lost someone or were about to lose someone. People who didn't know. She watched as a man with a grey appearance, wearing a bulky overcoat, sat hunched over his newspaper. He sighed every time he turned the page. Lorraine was just wondering what his story was, who he was here for, what sadness lay in his life like leaves in a river, when she noticed the print on the page he was reading. She stopped. She stared for a moment then she moved over to the man. Lorraine stood a breath away from him as she peered at the story in the newspaper.

Human bones found in woodland behind hotel. Workmen have discovered a human skeleton, believed to be a female, while carrying out landscaping work on an area of woodland behind a hotel. Forensic tests suggest that the remains are over 200 years old.

She'd been found. At last, after all these years, she'd been found. And maybe now it would be over.

Lorraine stepped from the hospital and made her way to the bus stop. It was cold but the sky was clear. The wind whipped the trees, still, and the clouds moved like slow ships. The season would falter yet, most probably, the winter wasn't quite done, but Lorraine could see and feel the future spring already close by. She'd always hated the winter, hated being cold, hated the layers she had to wear and the way it dried her skin. She couldn't wait for it to be at a close and for blue skies to roll through again. More than anything now, she wanted the sun to shine again. She wanted to walk with her shadow stretched out behind her, the dark mornings and the long nights in the past. She'd always hated the winter, and this year's had been particularly bad.

If you enjoyed *Out of the City*, why not try our other Armley Press titles available from Amazon and through UK bookshops?

Ray Brown: *In All Beginnings*
ISBN 0-9554699-6-1
Mark Connors: *Stickleback*
ISBN 0-9934811-2-3
A.J. Kirby: *The Lost Boys of Prometheus City*
ISBN 0-9934811-5-4
John Lake: *Hot Knife*
ISBN 0-9554699-1-6
John Lake: *Blowback*
ISBN 0-9554699-4-7
John Lake: *Speed Bomb*
ISBN 0-9554699-5-4
John Lake: *Amy and the Fox*
ISBN 0-9934811-0-9
M.W. Leeming: *Justice is Served*
ISBN 0-9934811-4-7
Mick McCann: *Coming Out as a Bowie Fan*
ISBN 0-9554699-0-2
Mick McCann: *Nailed*
ISBN 0-9554699-2-9
Mick McCann: *How Leeds Changed the World*
ISBN 0-9554699-3-0
Chris Nickson: *Leeds, the Biography*
ISBN 0-9554699-7-8
Nathan O'Hagan: *The World is (Not) a Cold Dead Place*
ISBN 0-9554699-9-2
Nathan O'Hagan: *Out of the City*
ISBN 0-978-0-9934811-6-1
Samantha Priestley: *Reliability of Rope*
ISBN 0-9554699-8-5
David Siddall: *Breaking Even*
ISBN 0-9934811-1-6
K.D. Thomas: *Fogbow and Glory*
ISBN 0-9934811-3-0

Visit us at www.armleypress.com and look for Armley Press on Facebook and Twitter

Lightning Source UK Ltd.
Milton Keynes UK
UKHW01f1009280618
324894UK00002BA/159/P